THE FABER BOOK
OF
NURSERY STORIES

anthologies edited by Barbara Ireson

THE FABER BOOK OF NURSERY VERSE

VERSE THAT IS FUN

COME TO THE FAIR

retold by Barbara Ireson

THE STORY OF THE PIED PIPER

THE GINGERBREAD MAN

THE FABER BOOK OF NURSERY STORIES

edited by
BARBARA IRESON

illustrated by
SHIRLEY HUGHES

→ FABER CLASSICS ←

First published in 1966
by Faber and Faber Limited
Bloomsbury House
74–77 Great Russell Street
London WC1B 3DA

This edition published in 2013

Typeset by Faber and Faber
Printed in England by TJ International

The right of Barbara Ireson and Shirley Hughes to be identified as editor and illustrator of this work respectively has been asserted in accordance with Section 77 of the Copyright, Designs and Patents Act 1988

A CIP record for this book
is available from the British Library

ISBN 978–0–571–30759–3

2 4 6 8 10 9 7 5 3 1

Introduction

The aim of this book is to produce a collection of stories which can be read both by and to young children. Each story has been chosen because it has been well-told, simply told, and, nearly always, briefly told.

My main preoccupation has been diversity, and apart from the two stories adapted from Hans Christian Andersen, each author is represented once only. There are more stories written for young children about animals than about any other subject and many in this collection have animal characters; but I have tried to choose the themes from as wide a range as possible. I have been careful to include folk tales, some of them little known, some of them old favourites, stories of magic and adventure, and stories about everyday things like umbrellas, helicopters, and building sites.

From the start this collection was conceived as a picture-story book with every story illustrated. Miss Shirley Hughes's drawings, which bring an imaginative and detailed interpretation to each one, will, I am certain, give constant pleasure not only to children reading for themselves, but also to those listening with the pictures before them.

BARBARA IRESON

Contents

Contents

BLACK BILL

Snowdrop was a white rabbit, white as snow. She had soft brown eyes and pink insides to her ears. She could do almost everything but talk, and that did not matter much. She could wrinkle her nose, flap her ears, and half-close her eyes. This was how she smiled, or frowned, or showed she was pleased.

Snowdrop lived in a wooden hutch. The front was made of wire netting, so she could look out. There was also a dark part with no window, filled with straw. This was her bedroom. She made herself a cosy hole in the middle of the straw, and slept with her nose resting on her fluffy, white paws.

The hutch was in a shed in the garden. The door of the shed was always left wide open, so she could see some trees, some bushes, and a path. She could see the sky as well. Better than trees, or bushes, or sky, was the sight of Susan, her mistress, running down the path calling, "Hallo, Snowdrop! Hallo, Snowdrop!" Then Snowdrop smiled her widest, sweetest smile. She belonged to Susan and loved her best in the world.

Susan was a little girl with long, fair pigtails. She took great care of Snowdrop, and never forgot to feed her. She gave her just the things rabbits like best, such as crisp lettuce, young carrots, and a tempting mash of tea-leaves and bran. She cleaned the hutch out every day, and put fresh straw in the bedroom on Saturdays.

Snowdrop was very happy. She had plenty to eat, plenty to watch, and plenty to think about.

One evening, when it was getting dark, Snowdrop had a visit from some wild rabbits who lived on the moor beyond the garden. They were a strange crowd, with untidy brown fur and bold eyes. They had a way of showing their sharp, pointed teeth when they spoke. They crept into the shed like shadows, jumped on to the wheelbarrow, and peeped into the hutch.

Snowdrop was glad there was strong wire netting between herself and the visitors. She trembled when they spoke in their loud, shrill voices, showing their sharp teeth. They asked a great many questions, and if she did not answer at once, they asked the questions again and again and again.

"What do you eat?"

"Where do you sleep?"

"What do you do all day long?"

"Aren't you tired of being shut up in a cage like a prison?"

Snowdrop did not think her cage was at all like a prison. It was like a home, but she was not brave enough to say so.

Just then, Dandy, the dog, barked, and the shadows stole away leaving her alone. She cuddled down in her cosy straw bed and tried to go to sleep, but she dreamed of loud, shrill voices, and sharp teeth.

The next evening, the wild rabbits came again. This time there was a black rabbit with them, named Black Bill. He told her stories of his life on the moors, and the fun he had with his friends.

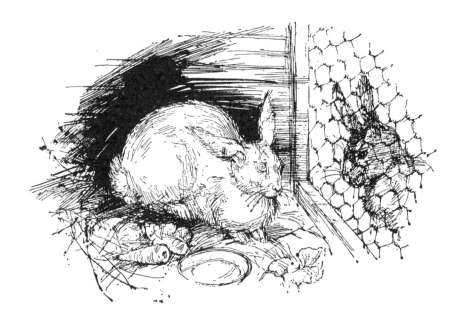

"No cage for me!" said Black Bill. "No food poked between the wire netting, smelling of human fingers. I eat what I choose. I nibble fresh green leaves with the dew on them, and tender shoots that melt in the mouth. Have you ever danced in the moonlight?"

"No," said Snowdrop sadly.

"Have you chased your shadow over the moors?"

"No," said Snowdrop again.

"Have you ever played leapfrog with a band of jolly companions?"

"No, never."

"Then why don't you join us?" Black Bill smiled in a cunning way and went on. "We will find you a snug burrow in the warren where we live, and show you the best feeding places. We will take care of you, and be your friends. What do you say?"

But Snowdrop was afraid of Black Bill, and too fond of Susan to want to run away.

The wild rabbits came again and told her more stories. Snowdrop listened. It would be nice to have a burrow all to herself, with a front door, a back door, and a soft, sandy floor. Then she could play with the other rabbits and run and jump on the wide, rolling moor. One evening she said timidly: "I will go with you, and just have a *look* at your home. I can come back to my hutch, if I want to."

"Of course you can. You can please yourself," said Black Bill, smiling and showing his teeth in a horrid way. Then, before Snowdrop could say "Carrots!" the wild rabbits were biting at the door of the hutch, and scratching with their strong claws. Soon the catch gave way, and the door swung open. She was pulled and pushed down the path, out of the garden.

It was a long way to the warren on the moor. Snowdrop was soon very tired. Her legs ached. Her head ached. Her feet were sore. She kept bumping into things and hurting herself. If she lagged behind, one of the wild rabbits gave her a prod in the back with a hard foot, or a nip on the ear with sharp teeth.

"Oh dear!" thought Snowdrop, tears running down her furry face. "Why did I leave my quiet, safe hutch?"

At last they reached the warren, which was a sandy hollow. It was full of rabbit holes, dozens and dozens of them.

"This is your burrow," growled Black Bill, pushing her into the entrance of a small, dark hole. She crept a little way down the tunnel. It was a horrid place,

cold and damp. It smelt of dead cabbage leaves. Indeed, it smelt more like a dustbin than a home.

Snowdrop was too tired to make any fuss. She fell asleep, with her nose resting on her tired paws.

The next morning, she woke up feeling stiff and hungry. "I am going home now," she said to Black Bill.

Then the wild rabbits burst out laughing, "Ha! Ha! Ha! He! He! He!" Black Bill laughed loudest of all.

"Go home!" he said, showing his teeth. "You'll never see your hutch again. You'll never find your way back. We shan't show you. You belong to us now."

"No, I don't!" cried Snowdrop. "I belong to Susan, and I wish I had never left her."

"Oh, no! You belong to us. You are our slave. Come on, you fellows! Roll her in the mud to start with. Whoever heard of a WHITE rabbit?"

They rolled her in the mud, and rolled her in the mud, until she was a dirty brown all over. Even the pink linings of her ears were brown.

"That is better," said Black Bill, looking at her. "Much better. Now you can set to work. You must do whatever we tell you."

They gave her so many different orders that she got very muddled. "Come here! Go there! Do this! Do that!"

Black Bill

Then she was set to clean out all the burrows, and carry away any rotten leaves and stalks. There were so many twists and turns in the tunnels that she often got lost, and however hard she worked, there always seemed some rubbish left in a dark corner. "Take this! Take that! Move this! Move that!" The unkind voices went on and on.

Her next job was to mind the rabbit babies. This was a little better, but not much. The babies would not keep still for a minute. They wriggled and squiggled like eels. If they squeaked, their mothers appeared, and scolded her for not taking proper care of their darlings.

Not one of the lovely things Black Bill had promised her came true. Not even one. She never nibbled tender shoots with the dew on them but only hard stalks left by the others.

She never danced in the moonlight.

She never chased her shadow over the moor with a band of jolly companions. She *had* no jolly companions. She was only a slave.

Snowdrop decided to run away. From the wild rabbits she had heard horrible stories about the dangers of the moor. There were stoats and weasels, whose teeth never let go, once they had met in a fierce bite. There were men with guns who shot rabbits from far away, so their wives could make them huge rabbit pies, with thick gravy and brown crusts. But she did not care. Better be a dinner for a family of hungry stoats or weasels, or even a pie for a man with a gun, than a slave to such cruel masters.

One morning, when the sun had made the other rabbits sleepy, Snowdrop crept out of the burrow she had been told to clean, and hopped quietly into the heather. She did not know which way to go, north or south, east or west. She just lifted her pink nose, and sniffed.

Among the smells of gorse and heather, dry grass and hot soil was a faint smell of home. That was the way she must go.

She set off at a steady trot-trot. The poor food the wild rabbits had given her had left her weak, but the work had hardened her soft pads. She saw the bees buzzing round the bells of the heather, and heard a lark singing, high above her, in the sky. "They are free," thought Snowdrop, "and I am free, too."

Her heart was beating as she ran, thud, thud, thud. Suddenly it beat so loudly that she felt frightened. Was it her heart thudding, or was it something else she could hear? Something behind her? The sound of running feet?

Snowdrop turned her head, and had one look over her shoulder. One look was enough. She saw a black shape racing after her, followed by some brown ones. It was Black Bill and his companions, hot on her trail.

13

Black Bill

How Snowdrop ran! Ears laid back flat, she sped like the wind. Home felt near. If only she could cross the last strip of bracken, and the sloping field, then she could dive through the fence into the safe garden.

She zig-zagged through the bracken and gained a little, as Black Bill lost sight of her under the tall, green leaves. But the open field had no cover, and he gained on her, muttering and hissing under his breath. Luckily she was so thin that she slipped between the posts of the fence easily, while plump Black Bill had to push and squeeze.

The garden seemed empty. There was not a friend in sight. No Susan. No Dandy the dog. Not even a squirrel. She made for the summer-house, and jumped over the door-step. Where could she hide?

There was a table with some chairs. Perhaps she could get under a cushion? Then she saw Susan's dolls' cradle on the floor, hung with white muslin curtains. Into this she sprang, burrowing under the sheets and blankets.

Rose, the talking doll, was already asleep in the cradle. Snowdrop landed on her middle, and she gave a loud and surprised, "Ma-ma! Ma-ma! Ma-ma!"

Black Bill heard the voice, and slunk away. Human beings had guns. Some had sticks and stones, or other things that could hurt. He would lie low for a while.

Susan was up the pear tree. She heard a scuffle. She heard Rose calling: "Ma-ma!

Ma-ma! Ma-ma!" She climbed down the tree, ran to the summer-house, and knelt beside the cradle. There was Rose, with her yellow wig and pink cheeks, and beside her were two long, brown ears.

Susan slid her hand very gently under the blankets. She felt fur. Then she felt the whiskers and paws of a warm, trembling body. She took it into her arms and began stroking the long ears. She whispered comforting words. "Poor little rabbit! Poor little frightened thing! I know you are my own lost Snowdrop, though you are so brown and dirty. I wish you could tell me where you have been. But I'll soon have you clean and white again."

First, Susan washed the mud off. Then she let Snowdrop dry in the sunshine. Last of all, she brushed her until she was like a soft, white snowball.

As Snowdrop sat in her hutch, with clean straw, and a tea of fresh lettuce and carrot, she was the happiest rabbit in the world.

Of course the wicked wild rabbits tried to get her back, but they never managed to harm her, as Dandy the dog kept watch near the shed. One growl—and they ran for their lives.

Dandy sent a message to Black Bill by a friendly crow, saying that if Black Bill came into the garden once more, Dandy would tear him into little pieces, and crunch his bones to powder.

This so frightened Black Bill and his friends, that none of them dared even poke a whisker through the fence, and Snowdrop lived in peace ever after.

RUTH AINSWORTH

THUMBELINA

Once there was a young wife who wanted a little daughter more than anything else in the world. She went to a fairy and asked her:

"Can you grant me just one wish? Can you give me a little girl?"

And the fairy said to the woman:

"Take this barleycorn seed, plant it in a flower pot and your wish will come true."

The young wife thanked the fairy and went home and did exactly as she had been told. At once, out of the pot there grew up a beautiful flower. It was a large yellow flower and its petals were tightly closed.

Thumbelina

Then, as the young wife watched, the petals unfolded and, in the centre of the flower, there sat a tiny little girl. This was the daughter the fairy had promised and the woman loved her straight away and called her Thumbelina because she was no bigger than her thumb.

She found half a walnut shell to make a bed for Thumbelina, and she gathered violet petals to make her a soft mattress, and rose petals for her covers.

Every day while the young wife was cooking and cleaning, Thumbelina stayed in her tiny walnut shell cradle safely on top of the table. As she worked the woman sang to her and told her stories and when the work was done they played together.

But one night a great big ugly toad hopped into the room and saw the beautiful little girl asleep in her walnut shell.

"She would make a fine wife for my son," the toad thought, and she carried sleeping Thumbelina away with her to her home in the river bank.

Her ugly son croaked for joy when he saw her.

"How lucky I am to have such a pretty wife," he said. But his croaking wakened Thumbelina and when she saw the two great toads staring at her, she was terrified.

"Take me home. Take me home," she cried.

But the toads said:

"No, you are going to stay here with us always."

In the morning, while they were making a home for her, they left her in her little walnut shell on a lily pad. Thumbelina looked up at the sky and out at the water and felt so lost and alone. She began to sob. Now some fish in the stream had heard the old Mother Toad talking to her son and they heard Thumbelina sobbing and were sorry for her. They swam to the lily pad and gnawed at the stem until they had gnawed right through it and the lily pad drifted away down the stream.

Thumbelina stopped sobbing. And, as she was carried further and further away from the toads, she began to feel happy again. The sun was shining and she lay in her tiny shell watching the clouds moving in the sky above her, watching the birds darting down to the water and away again, and watching the pretty butterflies who hovered near her.

A great cockchafer buzzed near her floating lily pad and hovered over her as she drifted down the stream. Suddenly he snatched her up out of her walnut shell and carried her away from the river, right over a meadow to a wood beyond. At first he was kind to her and gave her honey to eat, but when the lady-cockchafers saw her and laughed at her because she was so like a human, he no longer wanted her and he just left her all alone sitting on a daisy.

When it grew chilly towards evening and darkness spread through the wood, little Thumbelina began to cry again. She could see the birds flying back to their nests, and she could see lots of little animals who lived in the wood scurrying back to their homes, but she was far away from her home and she didn't know which way to go. A field-mouse, on her way back to her warm nest, heard Thumbelina and went up to her.

"What is the matter," she asked her, "and why are you all on your own in the wood?"

Thumbelina told the mouse everything that had happened to her and when she had finished the kind mouse said:

"Come to my nest and live with me. You can help me with the cleaning and the cooking and stay with me as long as you like."

So Thumbelina went with the field-mouse to her nest in a corn-field on the other side of the wood. The weeks went by quickly, for the mouse kept Thumbelina very busy, but she was happy and so she did not mind working hard. She would have stayed with the mouse, but one day a visitor came to the nest—a velvety black mole. He lived nearby and knew the field-mouse well. The mole stayed for a long time talking to the field-mouse and Thumbelina. He could not see Thumbelina for, like all moles, he was blind, but he loved the sound of her voice. After this he came again and again to talk to her.

He invited them to visit him in his burrow under the ground, and once when they went, Thumbelina saw a poor swallow lying in the dark passage that led to the mole's home. As they passed by the mole kicked the bird roughly out of the way, but Thumbelina waited behind and, thinking the poor bird was dead, she put a leaf over it. But when she bent near she heard its heart beating faintly and she knew the bird was still alive.

After this she went every day to take the swallow food and water, and every day she saw it was getting a little stronger. When the bird was well enough they talked together of the trees and the flowers and the blue skies where the bird would soon be flying again. But Thumbelina could not talk of these things without feeling sad because the mole, who had grown to love her sweet voice, had asked her to marry him and go to live in his burrow under the ground, away from the sunshine and the flowers. Every day that took the swallow nearer to his freedom took Thumbelina nearer to this new life with the mole which she dreaded. The field-mouse would not hear of Thumbelina's refusing to marry her neighbour, who was rich and had a fine home.

At last the day came for Thumbelina's wedding to the mole. She crept away to say good-bye to the swallow. Tears came into her eyes as she put her tiny arms around his neck and said:

"Good-bye, my friend, I shall always remember you."

The swallow saw how unhappy she was and he begged:

"Thumbelina, don't go to the mole. I think I'm strong enough to fly now. I might even be able to carry you on my back. Come with me, Thumbelina, to the flowers and the sunshine. You saved my life, now let me help you. I shall take you right away from here."

And he did. The swallow carried Thumbelina a long way from the mole and his burrow. He flew with her on and on until at last he came to a place where a carpet of golden flowers lay over a meadow. There the swallow put her gently down.

"Good-bye, sweet Thumbelina," he called to her as he flew off, "you will be happy here."

"Well," thought Thumbelina, "here I am again all alone and sitting in a flower." But she wasn't alone. Looking round she saw a little manikin, just about the same size as she was. He was sitting in another of the beautiful golden flowers and on his head he wore a golden crown. He bowed to her and came and took her hand in his.

"You are the loveliest girl I have ever seen," he said. "Will you stay here with me and be my Queen?"

Now Thumbelina knew why the swallow had brought her here and with great joy she said, "Yes." And a fairy came out of every flower in the meadow for the wedding of their King and Queen.

From that time on Thumbelina was never lonely again. She stayed in the golden meadow with her Flower King and they lived happily ever after.

Adapted from Hans Christian Andersen

THE UGLY DUCKLING

A mother duck once had four pretty fluffy ducklings and one more that was not so pretty. As time went by the four ducklings grew prettier and fluffier and the last one grew uglier and uglier. Mother Duck pretended not to notice this but one day another duck said to her:

"What a pity that fifth duckling of yours is so ugly! He doesn't look a bit like the others, does he?"

The four pretty ducklings overheard this and they began to tease the poor ugly one.

"You're not like us," they said. "Go away and play on your own."

This made the ugly duckling very sad and he would go off into a far corner of the farmyard and hide.

The Ugly Duckling

But when Mother Duck taught her ducklings to swim, it was the ugly duckling who learned quickest. After only one lesson he could swim faster and further than all the others. This made his brothers and sisters dislike him even more. Now they never let him join in their games. Whenever he went near them they pecked him and chased him off.

So one day the ugly duckling left the farmyard and went right away from them all. He went out on to the moors. There he saw some wild ducks.

"Perhaps they will be my friends," he thought, and he called to them. But the wild ducks cried out:

"Who are you, you ugly creature? You're not one of us. Go away."

And once again the ugly duckling hid himself because he was so miserable.

While he was hiding under a bush, he heard a most frightening sound—the 'crack', 'crack' of a gun. He shivered with fear. Worse was to come. Only a few feet from where he was hiding, a great gun dog went plunging through the

bushes. The ugly duckling did not dare to move. He stayed under the bush until it was dark and only then did he feel it was safe to come out.

He started off again not knowing where he was going, and then, shining through the darkness, he saw a light. It came from the open doorway of a cottage. The ugly duckling crept up to it. He could see a fire burning in the hearth. It looked welcoming. And an old woman was sitting there with a hen and a cat.

"Come in, little duckling," said the woman when she saw him. "Come and live with us and give me your eggs."

So the ugly duckling joined them in the cottage and at first the woman was kind to him even though the hen and the cat were not very friendly. But when two days had gone by and he had not laid her an egg, the old woman began to taunt him:

"When are you going to give me an egg, you ugly little creature?" she said.

And the hen said:

"What good are you? You cannot lay eggs as I can, and you're so odd-looking. You're no ornament to have around."

After this the ugly duckling no longer wanted to stay at the cottage. He went off on his own again and wandered a long, long way.

At last he came to a lake, it was pleasant there and he liked it among the reeds by the shore. That evening before it grew dark, he saw a flock of birds rise into the air from the water. They were birds he had never seen before, big beautiful birds. Their feathers were pure white and their wings were wide and powerful. He hid from them among the reeds in case they should call him ugly and tell him to go away.

The ugly duckling stayed there by the lake for months and months. He stayed right through the long cold winter when it was difficult to find food and sometimes there was ice on the water. He was lonely and often he was hungry and cold, but he stayed there all on his own, for he had nowhere else to go.

Then at last it began to get warmer and the leaves came on the trees and the water looked blue again. The ugly duckling felt the warm sunshine on his feathers and he swam right out into the middle of the lake where the water was still and as clear as a mirror.

There he saw himself reflected in the water. He stared. He didn't look like an ugly duckling. He stopped swimming and stared again. He couldn't believe what he saw. There in the water was one of those lovely white birds he had seen when he had first come to the lake. He spread his wings and the bird in the water spread enormous pure white wings, he waggled his neck and the bird in the water moved a long elegant neck to and fro.

The Ugly Duckling

At that moment he heard the sound of rippling water and looking up he saw the white birds gliding towards him. They came right up to him and their leader said:

"We have come to ask you to join us. You are the most handsome swan on this lake."

And the bird that had been an ugly duckling said:

"SWAN? Am I really a swan?"

And all the white birds said together:

"Of course you're a swan. Can't you see that you are just like us?"

Now at last the ugly duckling knew why he had never looked like his duckling brothers, and it did not matter now that he was a beautiful white swan.

"Yes, I will come with you," he said to the white birds. And with his lovely neck straight and his head held high he swam away to live with the swans. He belonged with them. He was never alone again.

Adapted from Hans Christian Andersen

THE BEST HOUSE

Peter was a white rabbit, and he lived in a big warm hutch by a sunny wall. He was very fat; he had pink eyes, and his ears sometimes stood straight up, and sometimes hung down like curtains.

"You are the best rabbit in the world, Peter," his mistress said to him one morning, when she was giving him his breakfast. But she did not know him very well.

"I am tired of my hutch," he thought to himself. "I am sure that there are interesting, exciting things happening outside in the world. I want to see them. I am tired of my hutch."

When she had finished giving him his breakfast, his mistress forgot to fasten the door of the hutch properly. Peter pretended that he did not notice, and went on nibbling his cabbage-stalk; but as soon as she had left him, he dropped the cabbage-stalk, hopped across to the door, and gave it a little push with his pink nose. He found that it opened quite easily, so he gave it another push, until it swung right back on its hinges and left a big gap for him to get through.

"Hurrah!" said Peter, sniffing the air and feeling very pleased with himself.

"Now I shall be able to see all the interesting, exciting things that are happening outside."

So he jumped down from his hutch, and went hopping off across the farmyard, with his ears flapping like curtains stirred by the wind.

He hopped to the door of Mrs Pig's sty.

"Good morning, Mrs Pig," said he, very politely. "Why do you not leave your house, and come with me to see all the interesting, exciting things that are happening outside?"

"Leave my house?" grunted Mrs Pig. "No, no, little rabbit, I will not leave my house. For here I am warm and comfortable, and well-fed, and if I go outside, who knows what will happen? Leave my house, indeed! Why, I have the best house in the whole farmyard! As for you, if you go much farther, Mr Fox will get you."

"I don't believe it!" said Peter crossly, and he hopped a little farther on to Mrs Cow's shed.

"Good morning, Mrs Cow," said he, very politely. "Why do you not leave your house, and come with me to see all the interesting, exciting things that are happening outside?"

"Leave my house?" lowed Mrs Cow. "No, no, little rabbit, I will not leave my house. For here I am warm and comfortable and well-fed, and if I go outside, who knows what will happen? Leave my house, indeed! Why, I have the best house in the whole farmyard. As for you, if you go much farther, Mr Fox will get you."

"I don't believe it!" said Peter crossly, and he hopped a little farther on till he came to Mrs Mare's stable.

"Good morning, Mrs Mare," said he, very politely. "Why do you not leave your house, and come with me to see all the interesting, exciting things that are happening outside?"

"Leave my house?" neighed Mrs Mare. "No, no, little rabbit, I will not leave my house. For here I am warm and comfortable and well-fed, and if I go outside before my master is ready for me, who knows what will happen to me? Leave my house indeed! Why, I have the best house in the whole farmyard. As for you, if you go much farther, Mr Fox will get you."

"I don't believe it," said Peter crossly, and he hopped a little farther until he came to Mrs Hen's coop.

"Good morning, Mrs Hen," said he, very politely. "Why do you not leave your house, and come with me to see all the interesting, exciting things that are happening outside?"

"Leave my house?" clucked Mrs Hen. "No, no, little rabbit, I will not leave my house. Why, I have the best house in the whole farmyard. For here I am warm and comfortable and well-fed, and if I go outside, Mr Fox is sure to get me. He will get you, too, if you go much farther."

"I don't believe it!" said Peter crossly, and he went on hopping until he came to the gate at the end of the farmyard—and there he stopped.

For, sitting under the hedge on the other side of the gate, was a gentleman in a red coat, with a long bushy tail, and when he saw Peter his eyes shone cruelly, and he showed his teeth in a hungry smile.

"Good morning, little rabbit," said he, very politely. "Why do you stand on that side of the gate, when so many interesting, exciting things are happening on this side? Come with me, and I will show you my house, which is the best in the world."

Now Peter guessed that this was Mr Fox, and he knew that the only exciting, interesting thing that was likely to happen to him if he passed through the gate was that he would be turned into Mr Fox's breakfast.

So he jumped round, right-about-face, and went hopping back across the farmyard, much quicker than he had come, and his ears flapped very quickly indeed. He did not stop hopping until he reached his hutch, and there he gave an extra big hop, and hid himself in the little compartment that was his bedroom.

"I will never go out and look for interesting, exciting things again," he said to himself, "for if I do Mr Fox will be sure to get me. Here I am warm and well-fed and comfortable—and safe. Why, I have the best house in the whole farmyard!"

ANONYMOUS

THE LITTLE GREY SHEEP

There was once a boy who lost his little grey sheep. He put on his coat and his hat, and took his big crook and went out to look for her.

He looked in the meadow. There he saw daisies, and he saw buttercups, and he saw a big yellow dandelion. But he did not see his little grey sheep.

The meadow said, "Your little grey sheep did not come this way. If she had, she would have eaten my grass."

The boy saw that the grass had not been eaten, so he went away and looked in the long, long lane.

There he saw two eggs in a nest. But he did not see his little grey sheep.

And the lane said, "Your little grey sheep did not come this way, for if she had, my thorn bushes would have caught some of her wool."

The boy saw there was no wool on the thorn bushes, so he went away and looked in the brook.

There he saw pebbles, and he saw fishes, and he saw a beautiful brown snail. But he did not see his little grey sheep.

And the brook said, "Your little grey sheep did not come this way, for if she had, she would have drunk some of my water."

The boy saw that the little grey sheep had not been there, so he went away and looked in the farmer's field.

There he saw black sheep and white sheep, and some that were grey. But his own little grey sheep was not there.

And the field said, "Your little grey sheep did not come this way, for I would have noticed a stranger."

So the boy walked on for a long way, till he came to the wise owl who lived in the barn.

And he said to the wise owl, "How shall I find my little grey sheep? I looked for her in the meadow, but she had not eaten the grass there. I looked for her in the long, long lane, but she had not caught her wool on the thorns. I looked for her by the brook, but she had not drunk the water. And she is not in the farmer's field."

The owl only said, "Go home, go home, go h-o-m-e."

So then the boy took his long crook again, and walked on and on and on, till he reached his home.

There was the little grey sheep waiting for him!

The little grey sheep had only walked twice around the garden—*trit-trot*, *trit-trot*.

When the boy was at the back gate, the little grey sheep had been at the front gate. When the boy was at the front gate, the little grey sheep had been at the back gate!

ANONYMOUS

THE OLD IRON POT

Once there was a rich man who lived in a beautiful house. He was by far the richest man in all the countryside, but he was also a greedy master. The people who worked for him were very poor, because he paid them small wages for their hard work.

Not far from the rich man's house there was a lowly cottage in which lived a poor old farmer and his wife. They had worked for the rich man for many years, but they had been able to save very little.

One day the farmer's wife said to her husband, "All our money is gone. The time has come for us to sell the cow."

"Sell the cow?" exclaimed the old man, thinking he had not heard aright. "Why, what shall we do without milk?"

"I don't know," answered the good wife, "but we must have a little money to live. The old cow should bring—oh, perhaps a hundred pounds."

The old farmer's eyes brightened and he said, "I'll drive her to market to-morrow morning."

Early next morning, he started to market, leading the cow.

"Be sure you get a good sum for her," his wife called out after him.

"I'll do my best," he replied.

The old man had not gone far along the highway when he met an odd-looking little man who asked, "How much is your cow worth?"

"One hundred pounds, I think," answered the old man.

"I'll give you this pot for her," said the stranger, holding up a three-legged iron pot which he carried on his arm.

The old man looked very much surprised and said, "That old pot is worth nothing to me."

Then up spoke the iron pot, saying, "Take me! Try me!"

When the old man heard the pot speak, he thought it surely must be a magic pot, so he agreed to the bargain and the exchange was made. But as the farmer returned to his cottage, he recalled his wife's parting words, "Be sure you get a good sum for her."

"I'd better take the pot to the barn," he thought.

So he took it to the barn and tied it in the stall. Then he went into the cottage.

"Did you sell the cow?" the old woman wanted to know.

The husband nodded his head. Then he said, "Come to the barn and see what I have got." He led the way, carrying a lantern, and his wife followed.

"Look in the stall," he said.

At first the old woman was very much puzzled, and when she saw nothing in the stall but an old iron pot, she grew angry and said, "Surely you did not trade our cow for *that*?"

Before the old man could answer, the iron pot spoke up and said:

> "*Take me in and scour me bright;*
> *Hang me over the firelight.*"

"You see—it's a magic pot," said the old man. "Let us do as it asks."

So they took the pot into the house and scoured it until it shone. The next morning the old woman hung it over the fire. Soon it became hot and cried out, "I skip, I skip!"

"Tell me where you skip," said the old woman.

> "*I skip, I skip, as fast as I can;*
> *I skip to the house of the very rich man.*"

Before the old wife could answer, the iron pot had bounded off the fire and jumped through an open window. She burst into a hearty laugh when she saw the little legs scampering down the road.

Now the cook in the rich man's house was troubled. She had made a rich plum pudding for dinner, but when she had tied it up in the pudding bag she found it was too large to go into the pot.

"What shall I do?" she said. "There's not a pot in the kitchen large enough to hold the master's pudding."

At that moment, through the open window and down upon the table jumped the old iron pot.

"Try me," it cried out.

"Indeed I will!" said the cook, and she popped the pudding into the pot.

Then the pot cried out, "I skip, I skip, I skip!"

"Tell me where you skip," said the servant.

> "*I skip, I skip, as fast as I can;*
> *I skip to the house of the very poor man.*"

32

Before the cook could catch her breath, the old pot was hopping along the road again.

The poor man's wife was wondering what she could get for dinner, when suddenly the iron pot jumped through the window and came to rest on the table.

"Well," she said, "I see that the old pot has brought us a fine plum pudding." Then she called her husband for the meal.

When the pudding was eaten, the wife scoured the pot and set it on the fire. In a little while she heard it cry out, "I skip, I skip, I skip!"

"Tell me where you skip," she said.

> *"I skip, I skip, as fast as I can;*
> *I skip to the barn of the very rich man."*

Out of the window leaped the old iron pot. The little legs pattered down the highway and across a meadow to the rich man's barn, where several men were threshing wheat.

"What shall we put the grain in?" asked one of the men. "The sacks from the village have not yet come."

"Here is an old iron pot," said another.

The men began to fill the iron pot with the wheat, and soon the pot held all the wheat the men had threshed.

"I skip, I skip, I skip!" cried the pot.

"Tell me where you skip," said a man.

> "*I skip, I skip, as fast as I can,*
> *I skip to the house of the very poor man.*"

And out of the barn door leaped the old iron pot. It skipped over the meadow and down the highway to the poor man's house. With a great bound it went through the window and stood in the middle of the kitchen where the old woman was working.

"Come and see what the old pot has brought us," the wife called to her husband.

"Why, it's full of fine wheat," said the old man. "Let's empty it."

"It will last us for a long time," the wife said, as they poured out bushels of the wheat.

The pot was scoured again as bright as silver and set on the fire. Then, some mornings later, as the old couple were eating breakfast, the pot again cried out, "I skip, I skip, I skip!"

"Where do you skip now?" they both asked, and the pot answered:

> "*I skip, I skip, as fast as I can,*
> *To the counting-house of the very rich man.*"

With a great bound, the pot leaped out of the window and pattered down the highway to the rich man's house.

On just that morning, the rich man was in his counting-house, where he kept all of his money. The table where he sat was covered with gold and silver coins. Suddenly something leaped through the open window and bumped against the table. It was the old iron pot, of course.

"Why, here's a good strong pot," he said. "It will do very nicely to hold some of my gold and silver."

He was surprised to find how much the old pot held, for indeed, he was able to pack *all* of his coins in it!

"I skip, I skip, I skip!" cried the pot.

The rich man jumped to his feet in alarm. Away leaped the pot out of the window and down the highway. It carried the money to the house of the poor man, who was standing in the kitchen.

Now it was his turn to call his wife. "Come quickly and see what the old pot has brought us!" he shouted. "Shining gold and silver! It's enough to last us to the end of our days!"

"Ah," said his wife when she saw the bright coins, "what a bargain you struck when you traded the cow for this pot! Now it need never skip again."

But as soon as all of the money had been taken out of the pot, the old man and his wife again heard it cry out, "I skip, I skip, I skip!"

"And where do you skip now?" asked the old wife.

But this time the pot did not stop to answer. It leaped out of the window and hurried down the highway. As it came down the road, the rich man's cook happened to see it, and promptly told her master about it.

The rich man ran as fast as he could to meet the pot. He threw his arms around it and cried, "I've caught you this time!"

But then the strangest thing happened. The handle of the iron pot wound itself around the rich man, tying him up!

"I skip, I skip, I skip!" the pot cried.

Then off it started, dragging the rich man down the road to the poor man's cottage. This time it did not stop. When it passed the kitchen, the farmer's wife called out of the window, "*Please* tell me where you skip!"

And the last words the pot spoke, as it carried off the greedy man, were:

"*I skip, I skip, as fast as I can,*
To the far North Pole with the very rich man!"

ANONYMOUS

THE CITY BOY AND THE COUNTRY HORSE

Once a little city boy named Johnny went with his mother and father to live on a farm.

Johnny felt very lonely. He had never been on a farm before. Everything was strange and new to him, and there was no one to play with. But the first morning, he woke up and the sun was shining and the birds were singing, and when he went outdoors in the clean sweet air, he felt very happy.

Johnny saw a little baby horse grazing in the grass. His brown coat gleamed in

35

the sun. When the little baby horse saw the little boy, he looked at him with such deep brown eyes that the little boy felt that he and the horse should be friends.

So Johnny went up to the white wooden fence and called to the horse, "Hey there!"

The baby horse, being a horse, thought the little boy had some hay for him Over he ran—gallop, gallop, gallop—up to the fence. He put his head overthe. fence and waited for his hay.

But Johnny did not have any hay for the baby horse.

The little horse thought, "This little boy has tricked me." He hung his handsome horse head and walked slowly away.

And when the little horse walked away and left Johnny standing alone on the other side of the fence, the little boy thought, "This little horse doesn't like me." He hung his little-boy head and walked away too, feeling lonelier than before.

The next day Johnny woke up bright and early, and the air smelled clean and good. His mother gave him a delicious hot breakfast, and the sun and the blue sky made the world look so beautiful that he was sure he could make friends with the baby horse.

"I'll try again today," Johnny thought.

So he went out to the pasture and called to the horse, "Hey there!"

The little horse thought, "He looks like such a fine little boy, I'm sure he won't trick me again." So he went running over to the fence on his slender legs— gallop, gallop, gallop.

But, of course, the little boy had no hay.

The little horse hung his head and walked away, swishing his tail from side to side in disappointment.

"That little boy tricked me," the little horse thought, "I can't be his friend."

When Johnny saw the baby horse walking away he hung his little-boy head and tears came to his eyes.

"That little horse still doesn't like me," he thought.

And more than anything, Johnny wanted to be friends with the little horse.

So the next morning, while he was eating his breakfast, he asked his mother a question.

"How do you make someone like you who doesn't know you?"

His mother asked him a question.

"How *can* you make someone like you if he doesn't know you?"

The little boy started to think.

"Then how can I make the little horse know me?" he wondered.

"What do little baby horses eat?" he asked.

His mother smiled.

"Horses eat carrots and oats and hay," she said. "There's lots of hay behind the barn."

Johnny swallowed his last bit of cereal and gulped down his last swallow of milk, and ran out of the house. He filled his arms with the hay he found behind the barn. Then he ran to the pasture as fast as he could.

"Little horse!" he called.

When the little horse heard him, he lifted up his head and thought, "Today he doesn't call and pretend he has some hay. Today we *might* make friends." And he came running over on his long, spindly legs—gallop, gallop, gallop.

And there was the little boy with an armful of hay.

The little horse ate it gratefully. He munched each wisp, shaking his head with every mouthful. Then he nuzzled the little boy with his velvety nose and licked the little boy's hand with his rough wet tongue.

Since the little horse couldn't talk, Johnny never knew why they had not been friends right from the start. He put his arms around the horse's head and rubbed his face back and forth against the short, stiff horse fur. He and the little baby horse were friends at last.

They grew up together and they had many good times. Johnny never again thought that someone who didn't know him didn't like him.

Anonymous

PHILLIPIPPA

Phillipippa was the kitchen-maid in King Carraway's palace. She washed the royal dishes, peeled the royal potatoes, and swept the red-tiled floor of the royal kitchen.

She did many other things besides these, but it would take far too long to write them all down here.

One morning the cook sent her to market to buy a new broom.

Phillipippa

"That old one is a perfect disgrace to the royal household; you must have a new one at once," said she crossly.

"Yes, Ma'am," replied Phillipippa; "I'll go at once."

She always said Ma'am when speaking to the cook, as it helped to keep her in a good temper. Phillipippa was very tactful.

The cook was fat. Her cotton print dresses were so tight that they looked as if the buttons might burst at any moment. Phillipippa felt quite nervous about it sometimes.

It didn't take her very long to get to the market-place. She tried several stalls, but couldn't buy a broom anywhere. They had all sold out. Phillipippa stood in the middle of the market square and debated what to do. She dare not go back to the royal palace without a broom. It was very awkward indeed.

Just at that moment along came a pedlar, and under his arm was the most beautiful broom Phillipippa had ever set eyes upon!

"Oh! what a love!" she exclaimed. "Please, is it for sale?"

"Yes," said the pedlar. He didn't tell her that he had picked it up in the road that very morning!

Phillipippa bought the broom and hurried back to the royal palace as fast as she could go.

"My word! what a time you've been!" said the cook.

"Indeed, Ma'am, I——"

"That is quite enough from you, Miss, thank you. And don't stand there staring either; anybody would think we had nothing to do. Come and sweep up the kitchen at once! I've been making the stuffing for the royal goose, and the crumbs have gone all over the floor." The cook snatched up an oven-cloth and banged a saucepan down on the fire with a bump, so that the coals scattered in all directions!

"My! *what* a temper she's got!" thought Phillipippa.

She picked up her new broom and began sweeping the floor. Over the red tiles flew the new broom, swish, swish! She had no sooner begun than she had finished! Phillipippa stared in amazement. What a wonderful broom it was! So light! She had never swept the kitchen floor as quickly as *that* before! It must be enchanted!

"Well, if that isn't luck!" thought Phillipippa. "We're going to be great friends, I can see," she said, patting the broom handle affectionately.

Next day, quite early, a little old woman came knocking at the kitchen door.

Phillipippa was sweeping round the royal larder. She unfastened the door.

Phillipippa

"Good morning to you, Miss," said the little old woman. "May I ask what you are doing with my broom?"

"*Your* broom?" cried the astonished Phillipippa. "Why, I bought it myself in the market yesterday."

"So you may have," replied the old woman angrily, "but I tell you it's *my* broom, just the same."

"Well, and what about me?" the broom asked suddenly in a little, high, squeaky voice.

Phillipippa was so surprised that she let go the broom handle with a jerk. It didn't fall over, but stood up all by itself in the middle of the floor!

"Come home *at once*," cackled the witch. "How *dare* you run away like that!"

"You run away yourself," piped the broom; "you horrid old woman! I'm quite happy where I am, thank you."

"Oh, are you?" cried the witch. "We'll soon see who is the master here!"

"Oh, shall we?" retorted the broom, and it shook all over with rage. "Go away at once," it squeaked, "or I'll sweep you out!"

"I don't think I should do that," said Phillipippa, beginning to feel quite alarmed.

But she had no sooner spoken, than the broom began sweeping as hard as it could go. Out of the royal kitchen it swept the old woman, and across the court-yard, so that she had to pick up her petticoats and run. Swish, swish, swish!

Over the drawbridge ran the witch, with the broom close at her heels.

And then, all of a sudden, the broom was back again in Phillipippa's hand, just as if nothing at all had happened! And as for the little old woman, she was no-where to be seen!

"Well, if that isn't strange!" thought Phillipippa. But she never said one word about it to anybody.

ANONYMOUS

THE THREE RATS

In a funny little hole under an old oak tree there lived three rats. Their names were Pick, Peck, and Puck. They were very quaint and pretty, as their heads and front feet were white, and their tails and back legs were black. They were so much alike that even their mother could not tell them apart.

Pick and Peck were always quarrelling, but Puck was a good little fellow. One day, when Pick and Peck were unusually bad-tempered, Puck said, "This hole is too small for three of us; I will go and find somewhere else to live."

Off he scampered, and ran for a long long time until he came to a pretty little cottage.

"I wonder who lives here," he said, as he ran up the garden path and squeezed under the door into the cosiest of kitchens. "Just the sort of place where you expect to find a cat," he thought, and he hid himself under the hearth-rug.

Pick and Peck, left by themselves, quarrelled so much that Peck said, "This hole is too small for two of us; I will find somewhere else to live."

Off he scampered, and ran for a long long time until he too came to the cottage.

"I wonder who lives here," he said, as he ran up the garden path and squeezed under the door into the cosy kitchen. "Just the sort of place where you expect to find a cat," he thought, and he hid himself in a teapot on the dresser.

Pick, left to himself, felt very lonely. "This hole is too big for one," he thought, "so I will find somewhere else to live."

Off he scampered, and ran for a long long time until he too came to the pretty cottage.

"I wonder who lives here," he said, as he ran up the garden path and squeezed under the door into the cosy kitchen. "Just the sort of place where you expect to find a cat," he thought, and he hid himself behind the clock on the mantel-shelf.

Soon after the kitchen door opened and a man came in, followed by a large black cat. The man's name was Mike. "We will make some tea," he said. As he lifted the teapot from the dresser out popped Peck.

"What an odd-looking rat!" said Mike. "I will take you to the Big Field, for if you stay here Puss will eat you."

He slipped Peck into his pocket and going out of the cottage, walked two miles to the East. On coming to the Big Field he took Peck from his pocket and let him run away.

Not long after he returned to the cottage he glanced at the clock and saw Pick peeping out.

"Good gracious," cried Mike, thinking Pick was Peck, "I thought I left you in the Big Field; you must have followed me home. If you stay here Puss may eat you, so I will take you to the Small Field."

So saying he slipped Pick into his pocket and going out of the cottage, walked two miles to the West. On coming to the Small Field he took Pick from his pocket and let him run away; then he plodded back to his cottage.

He had not been in the kitchen many minutes when by chance he stood on Puck, who was hidden under the hearth-rug. Puck squeaked, and Mike, lifting the corner of the rug, picked him up.

"You have followed me home two miles from the Big Field, and you have followed me home two miles from the Small Field," he said, "so now you shall stay with me for always, and Puss must promise never to eat you."

Puck was such a good little fellow that he and Puss were soon the best of friends, and they both lived happily with Mike all their lives.

ANONYMOUS

43

PETE AND THE WHISTLE

One hot sunny day, when Pete's shadow looked much blacker than usual, and followed him around wherever he went, Pete found a crowd of men at the end of his street. They had nothing on but their work-trousers and plimsolls, and they were digging, digging, digging, in the hot sun.

"What are you doing?" asked Pete.

"We're building a house," said one of them.

Pete was quiet for a minute. Then he said: "Tell me what you're *really* doing."

"We're building a house," said the man again. "Honestly we are."

Now Pete was very angry.

"But houses go up, not down," he cried. "You can't *dig* a house. You can dig potatoes, or worms, or something that you hid there last time, but how can you dig a house! *What* are you doing? Tell me!"

"Well," said the man, "if you'll listen very carefully—and very quietly—and leave my spade alone—I'll explain to you." And he wiped his hands on his trousers, for they were feeling rather sore and sticky.

And because Pete could see that what the man was going to tell him would be the truth, he stopped being angry and listened.

"Now, this hole here," said the man, "this hole that we're digging, is for standing the house in. When we build the wall of the house, we start it inside the hole, so that it stands up strong and steady.

"Why, if we built the wall right on top of the ground, without digging this hole first, as soon as the wind came along it'd blow the whole lot flat. One puff, and there'd be no house left."

"Like the three little pigs?" said Pete. "Like '*I'll huff and I'll puff*'?"

"That's right," said the man. " '*I'll huff and I'll puff and I'll blow your house down*.' That's why we have to dig a hole for the walls to stand in."

And he took up his spade again, and went on digging. And Pete went on watching.

When Pete thought he had seen enough of how the digging looked from one side, he thought he would see how it looked from the other side. So he jumped

44

across the hole, because it was still only a little one. And his shadow jumped too.

But Pete's shadow was a silly. It fell in the hole.

"Dig my shadow!" shouted Pete. So the men took up a spadeful of Pete's shadow, and tried to lift it up and put it near Pete. But the shadow fell off the spade and lay in the hole again. "Bother," said Pete. And the man said nothing because he was very hot; he just went on working.

Pete wanted to help. He said to the man: "I'm a jolly good digger. I dig jolly fast. Shall I help?"

But the man said "No!"

"No *thank you*, you mean," said Pete sadly.

"No thank you," said the man, and went on digging.

45

Pete and the Whistle

Suddenly, just behind him, a terrible noise started. It was like the noise a giant motor-bike would make. It made all the ground shake.

Pete turned round quickly. He saw a man working a machine which made a hole in the ground. The man had a loose pullover on and it shivered when the man's arms shivered with the machine.

"Can I do that?" said Pete, but the machine shouted louder than Pete—and the man did not hear a word.

Now another man came by, pushing a wheelbarrow. He filled it full of bricks, then he pushed it away.

When he came again, Pete said: "I can do that. I can put the bricks in. I'm jolly strong."

"All right," said the man. "You can help. But you must be very careful not to drop one on your toe."

" 'Course I won't," said Pete scornfully. "Shall I show you how I won't? I'll walk like this." And he put his heels together and turned his toes out, so that a brick would fall in the space between, and he walked like Charlie Chaplin. "Now I can't drop a brick on my toe, can I?" he said. And the man said, no, he couldn't.

So the three of them filled up the barrow, the man, and Pete, and Pete's shadow. At least, Pete's shadow *seemed* to be helping, even though he didn't make the barrow any fuller. And when the bricks were tidily piled together, and there was no room for any more, the man said to Pete, "You can ride on top."

"Really and truly?" said Pete.

"Really and truly, and absolooly," said the man.

"You mean absolutely," said Pete, laughing.

"So I do," said the man.

Then Pete sat on top of the bricks and the man pushed it.

It was the first time Pete had ridden on a barrow full of bricks. It was a bit knobbly, but not very, because the bricks were piled very tidily.

As for Pete's shadow, there was no room for it on the barrow. So it sat on the ground and pretended it was having a ride in a different barrow, with black bricks in it.

When Pete got off the wheelbarrow, an enormous machine had started work-ing. It was shovelling up sand in one place, and piling it up in another. It was very big and very clever and very quick.

Pete watched it for awhile, and thought. Then he put his hand in his pocket and took out a whistle. He threw it on the ground and waited. The machine won't want my whistle, he thought. I wonder what it will do.

46

Pete and the Whistle

But the machine didn't care. Quick as a wink, it picked up the whistle. Then it emptied it on the pile of sand.

"Don't do that!" shouted Pete angrily to the machine. And he ran as fast as he could to get his whistle back. But a man grabbed him by his overalls, and held him tight.

The man was very cross.

"That's a very silly thing to do," he shouted. "You might get a whole load of sand on top of you. Go away at once."

"Let go of me," cried Pete. "I want my whistle! You're pinching me! That machine's taken my whistle and I want it back. Look at it, look!"

The man looked. And just as he looked, the machine dropped another load of sand right on top of Pete's whistle.

"There now," said Pete bitterly. "Look what it's done. Beastly old machine! And it's your fault for stopping me getting it." And he put his thumb in his mouth, because he was very unhappy.

"Well," said the man, holding Pete very firmly, "we can't get it now. It'll be made into cement soon, and used to build the house."

"My whistle will?"

"That's right," said the man. "And when this house is built, and people are living in it, with curtains up at all the windows and smoke coming out of the chimney, then you can say to everyone, 'That house is sitting on my whistle'!"

"Yes," said Pete, brightening up. "That's what I'll say. I'll say, 'Get off my whistle, house, or I'll push you over'!"

He thought for a minute, then he said: "Will my whistle always be underneath the house? For ever and ever?"

"For ever and ever," said the man.

"Then it'll get spoilt," said Pete. "It won't be nearly so good when the house has been sitting on it."

"No," agreed the man, "it won't be so good for *whistling*. But it'll be very good for telling people about."

"Yes," said Pete, "it will be good for telling." He thought for a bit. Then he said: "I'll start telling people now."

And he tramped away over the bumpy ground, by the heaps of bricks, and the sand, and the wheelbarrows, and all the men in their dusty working trousers. And his shadow walked behind and fell in all the holes because it never looked where it was going.

"Silly old shadow," said Pete.

Then he said: "I'm glad *I'm* not made into cement. I'm glad the house won't be sitting on *me*. *Jolly* glad!" And he nodded his head to himself.

And away he ran.

That was another good day! LEILA BERG

THE BOY WHO GROWLED AT TIGERS

Once upon a time there was a little Indian boy whose name was Sudi, who growled at tigers.

"You be careful," his mother told him. "Tigers don't like being growled at."

But Sudi didn't care and, one day, when his mother was out shopping, he went for a walk to find a tiger to growl at.

He hadn't gone very far when he saw one hiding behind a tree waiting for him to come along so that he could chase him.

As soon as Sudi came up the tiger sprang out and growled, "GRRRRR-GRRRRRRGRRRRGRRRRRRRR." And Sudi growled right back, "GRRRR GRRRRRRGRRRRRGRRRRRRRR."

The tiger *was* annoyed!

"What does he think I am?" he thought. "A squirrel? A rabbit? A ocelot? Er . . . an ocelot?"

So next day, when he saw Sudi coming, he sprang out from behind the tree and growled louder than ever, "GRRRRRRGRRRRRRGRRRRRRGRRRRR-GRRRRRRGRRRRRRGRRRRRR!!!!!!!!"

"Nice tiger!" said Sudi, and stroked him.

The tiger couldn't bear it and went away and sharpened his claws and lashed his tail and practised growling.

"I *am* a tiger!" he said. "T-I-G-E-R; TIGER, GRRRRRR!" And then he went and had a drink at the pond. When he had finished he looked at his reflection in the water. There he was, a lovely yellow tiger with black stripes and a long tail. He growled again, so loudly that he frightened even himself, and ran away. At last he stopped.

"What am I running away for?" he thought. "It's only me. Oh dear, that boy has upset me! I wonder why he growls at tigers?"

Next day, when Sudi passed, he stopped him.

"Why do you growl at tigers?" he said.

"Well," said Sudi, "it's because I'm shy, really. And if I growl at tigers it sort of makes up for it, if you see what I mean."

"I see!" said the tiger.

"After all," said Sudi, "tigers are the fiercest animals in the world and it's very brave to growl at them."

The tiger *was* pleased.

"Fiercer than lions?" he said.

"Oh, yes!" said Sudi.

"And bears?"

"Much fiercer."

The tiger purred and felt very friendly.

"You *are* a nice boy!" he said and gave him a lick.

After that they often went for walks together and growled at each other.

DONALD BISSET

THE TRAVELS OF CHING

In the land of China a dollmaker made a little doll. The doll's name was Ching.

The dollmaker stuffed Ching with the best stuffing and glued him with the best glue. He sewed him with the best thread. Then he sold him.

He sold him to a toyshop where everything was very expensive. For a long time Ching sat in the toyshop and waited. He was waiting for somebody who wanted him.

Now there was a little Chinese girl who came by the toyshop. This little girl wanted Ching. But she was poor. She wanted Ching more than anything. But she had no money to buy him.

So Ching was sold to a rich tea merchant who drove away with him in his rickshaw.

But the tea merchant did not want Ching. He only bought him to give to somebody else.

He took Ching to the Post Office and sent him far, far away.

He sent Ching down a mountain on a donkey, and down a river in a sailing boat and across the ocean on a steamship, all the way to AMERICA.

There he was put on a train and sent across America to a city, where the post-man delivered Ching to a little girl who lived in a beautiful flat.

But the little girl did not want Ching. She already had more dolls and dresses and things than she knew what to do with.

She took Ching to the terrace and left him sitting right on the edge of the balustrade. It was a very careless thing to have done.

Ching fell off.

Luckily he floated down.

He landed on a small tree in a small back yard—and hung there. Then he dropped into a flower bed—and sat there.

When it rained, Ching got wet.

When it snowed, Ching got cold.

At last, in the spring, an old gentleman found him sitting in the flower bed. He was a nice old gentleman and took Ching inside.

But the old gentleman did not like Ching. What he liked was old chairs and old tables and old pieces of bric-à-brac.

He did not care for a dirty little doll.

So the old gentleman gave Ching to his cook. But the cook did not like Ching. Her kitchen was very neat and she did not like it cluttered.

She threw Ching into the rubbish bin.

Many people went by. But nobody wanted Ching. He was too dirty.

Early in the morning the dustman came and dumped Ching into his dust cart.

But the dustman did not want Ching. What he wanted was old bones and rags and old paper and old tin cans.

The dustman took Ching to his rubbish yard, but he had to put him in a separate place all by himself.

One day a Chinese laundryman came by and bought Ching. All the dustman charged for him was sixpence. IMAGINE!

The laundryman took Ching to his laundry and combed his hair. He washed his robe and ironed it. He went to a lot of trouble.

But the laundryman did not want Ching. He only bought him to give to somebody else.

He took Ching to the Post Office and sent him far, far away.

He sent Ching across America on a train, and across the ocean on a steamship, and up a river in a sailing boat, and up a mountain on a donkey, all the way to his little niece in CHINA!

And this little girl DID want Ching!

She had always wanted Ching, more than anything, ever since she saw him in a toyshop.

Do you remember?

She put him in her little cart and took him for a nice ride over her favourite bridge.

In the evening she and Ching had supper in the cosy kitchen.

Then they went to bed.

Outside a wise old Chinese owl looked in and the moon shone. The cat slept on the sill.

The little girl put her arm around Ching because she was so glad to have him.

ROBERT BRIGHT

MILLY-MOLLY-MANDY FINDS A NEST

Once upon a time, one warm summer morning, Uncle came quickly in at the back door of the nice white cottage with the thatched roof and shouted from the kitchen: "Milly-Molly-Mandy!"

Milly-Molly-Mandy, who was just coming downstairs carrying a big bundle of washing for Mother, called back, "Yes, Uncle?"

"Hi! quick!" said Uncle, and went outside the back door again.

Milly-Molly-Mandy couldn't think what Uncle wanted with her, but it had such an exciting sound she dropped the big bundle on the stairs in a hurry and ran down to the passage. But when she got to the passage she thought she ought not to leave the big bundle on the stairs, lest someone trip over it in the shadow; so she ran back again in a hurry and fetched the big bundle down, and ran along to

55

the kitchen with it. But she was in such a hurry she dropped some things out of the big bundle and had to run back again and pick them up.

But at last she got them all on to the kitchen table, and then she ran out of the back door and said, "Yes, Uncle? What is it, Uncle?"

Uncle was just going through the meadow gate, with some boards under one arm and the tool-box on the other. He beckoned to Milly-Molly-Mandy with his head (which was the only thing he had loose to do it with), so Milly-Molly-Mandy ran after him down the garden path to the meadow.

"Yes, Uncle?" said Milly-Molly-Mandy.

"Milly-Molly-Mandy," said Uncle, striding over the grass with his boards and tool-box, "I've found a nest."

"What sort of a nest?" said Milly-Molly-Mandy, hoppity-skipping a bit to keep up with him.

"Milly-Molly-Mandy," said Uncle, "I rather think it's a Milly-Molly-Mandy nest."

Milly-Molly-Mandy stopped and stared at Uncle, but he strode on with his boards and tool-box as if nothing had happened.

Then Milly-Molly-Mandy began jumping up and down in a great hurry and said, "What's a Milly-Molly-Mandy nest, Uncle? What's it like, Uncle? Where is it, Uncle? DO-O tell me!"

"Well," said Uncle, "you ought to know what a Milly-Molly-Mandy nest is, being a Milly-Molly-Mandy yourself. It's up in the big old oak-tree at the bottom of the meadow."

So Milly-Molly-Mandy tore off to the big old oak-tree at the bottom of the meadow, but she couldn't see any sort of a nest there, only Uncle's ladder leaning against the tree.

Uncle put the boards and tool-box carefully down on the ground, then he settled the ladder against the big old oak-tree, then he picked up Milly-Molly-Mandy and carried her up the ladder and sat her on a nice safe branch.

And then Milly-Molly-Mandy saw there was a big hollow in the big old oak-tree (which was a very big old oak-tree indeed). And it was such a big hollow that Uncle could get right inside it himself and leave quite a lot of room over.

"Now, Milly-Molly-Mandy," said Uncle, "you can perch on that branch and chirp a bit while I put your nest in order."

Then Uncle went down the ladder and brought up some of the boards and the tool-box, which he hung by its handle on a sticking-out bit of branch. And Milly-Molly-Mandy watched while Uncle measured off boards and sawed them and fitted them and hammered nails into them, until he had made a beautiful flat floor in the hollow in the big old oak-tree, so that it looked like the nicest little fairy-tale room you ever saw!

Then he hoisted Milly-Molly-Mandy off the branch, where she had been chirping with excitement like the biggest sparrow you ever saw (only that you never saw a sparrow in a pink-and-white striped cotton frock), and heaved her up into the hollow.

And Milly-Molly-Mandy stood on the beautiful flat floor and touched the funny brown walls of the big old oak-tree's inside, and looked out of the opening on to the grass down below, and thought a Milly-Molly-Mandy nest was the very nicest and excitingest place to be in the whole wide world!

Just then whom should she see wandering along the road at the end of the meadow but little-friend-Susan!

"Susan!" called Milly-Molly-Mandy as loud as ever she could, waving her arms as hard as ever she could. And little-friend-Susan peeped over the hedge.

At first she didn't see Milly-Molly-Mandy up in her nest, and then she did, and she jumped up and down and waved; and Milly-Molly-Mandy beckoned, and little-friend-Susan ran to the meadow-gate and couldn't get it open because she was in such a hurry, and tried to get through and couldn't because she was too big, and began to climb over and couldn't because it was rather high. So at last she squeezed round the side of the gate-post through a little gap in the hedge and came racing across the meadow to the big old oak-tree, and Uncle helped her up.

And then Milly-Molly-Mandy and little-friend-Susan sat and hugged themselves together, up in the Milly-Molly-Mandy nest.

Just then Father came by the big old oak-tree, and when he saw what was going on he went and got a rope and threw up one end to Milly-Molly-Mandy. And then Father tied an empty wooden box to the other end, and Milly-Molly-Mandy pulled it up and untied it and set it in the middle of the floor like a little table.

Then Mother, who had been watching from the gate of the nice white cottage

with the thatched roof, came and tied an old rug to the end of the rope, and little-friend-Susan pulled it up and spread it on the floor like a carpet.

Then Grandpa came along, and he tied some fine ripe plums in a basket to the end of the rope, and Milly-Molly-Mandy pulled them up and set them on the little table.

Then Grandma came across the meadow bringing some old cushions, and she tied them to the end of the rope, and little-friend-Susan pulled them up and arranged them on the carpet.

Then Aunty came along, and she tied a little flower vase on the end of a rope, and Milly-Molly-Mandy pulled it up and set it in the middle of the table. And now the Milly-Molly-Mandy nest was properly furnished, and Milly-Molly-Mandy was in such a hurry to get Billy Blunt to come to see it that she could hardly get down from it quickly enough.

Mother said, "You may ask little-friend-Susan and Billy Blunt to tea up there if you like, Milly-Molly-Mandy."

So Milly-Molly-Mandy and little-friend-Susan ran off straight away, hoppity-skip to the Moggs's cottage (for little-friend-Susan to ask Mrs Moggs's permission), and to the village to Mr Blunt's corn-shop (to ask Billy Blunt), while Uncle fixed steps up the big old oak-tree, so that they could climb easily to the nest.

And at five o'clock that very afternoon Milly-Molly-Mandy and little-friend-Susan and Billy Blunt were sitting drinking milk from three little mugs and eating slices of bread-and-jam and gingerbread from three little plates, and feeling just as excited and comfortable and happy as ever they could be, up in the Milly-Molly-Mandy nest!

JOYCE LANKESTER BRISLEY

THE LITTLE HALF-CHICK

There was once upon a time a Spanish Hen, who hatched out some nice little chickens. She was much pleased with their looks as they came from the shell. One, two, three, came out plump and fluffy; but when the fourth shell broke, out came a little half-chick! It had only one leg and one wing and one eye! It was just half a chicken.

The Little Half-Chick

Then Hen-mother did not know what in the world to do with the queer little Half-Chick. She was afraid something would happen to it, and she tried hard to protect it and keep it from harm. But as soon as it could walk the little Half-Chick showed a most headstrong spirit, worse than any of its brothers. It would not mind, and it would go wherever it wanted to; it walked with a funny little hoppity-kick, hoppity-kick, and got along pretty fast.

One day the little Half-Chick said, "Mother, I am off to Madrid, to see the King! Good-bye."

The poor Hen-mother did everything she could think of to keep him from doing so foolish a thing, but the little Half-Chick laughed at her naughtily. "I'm for seeing the King," he said; "this life is too quiet for me." And away he went, hoppity-kick, hoppity-kick, over the fields.

When he had gone some distance the little Half-Chick came to a little brook that was caught in the weeds and in much trouble.

"Little Half-Chick," whispered the Water, "I am so choked with these weeds that I cannot move; I am almost lost, for want of room; please push the sticks and weeds away with your bill and help me."

"The idea!" said the little Half-Chick. "I cannot be bothered with you; I am off to Madrid, to see the King!" And in spite of the brook's begging, he went away, hoppity-kick, hoppity-kick.

A bit farther on, the Half-Chick came to a Fire, which was smothered in damp sticks and in great distress.

"Oh, little Half-Chick," said the Fire, "you are just in time to save me. I am almost dead for want of air. Fan me a little with your wing, I beg."

"The idea!" said the little Half-Chick. "I cannot be bothered with you; I am off to Madrid to see the King!" And he went laughing off, hoppity-kick, hoppity-kick.

When he had hoppity-kicked a good way, and was near Madrid, he came to a clump of bushes, where the Wind was caught fast. The Wind was whimpering, and begging to be set free.

"Little Half-Chick," said the Wind, "you are just in time to help me; if you will brush aside these twigs and leaves, I can get my breath; help me, quickly!"

"Ho! the idea!" said the little Half-Chick. "I have no time to bother with you. I am going to Madrid, to see the King." And he went off, hoppity-kick, hoppity-kick, leaving the Wind to smother.

After a while he came to Madrid and to the palace of the King. Hoppity-kick, hoppity-kick, the little Half-Chick skipped past the sentry at the gate, and hoppity-kick, hoppity-kick, he crossed the court. But as he was passing the windows of the kitchen the Cook looked out and saw him.

"The very thing for the King's dinner!" she said. "I was needing a chicken!" And she seized the little Half-Chick by his one wing and threw him into a saucepan of water on the fire.

The Water came over the little Half-Chick's feathers, over his head, into his eyes. It was terribly uncomfortable. The little Half-Chick cried out,

"Water, don't drown me! Stay down, don't come so high!"

But the Water said, "Little Half-Chick, little Half-Chick, when I was in trouble you would not help me," and came higher than ever.

Now the Water grew warm, hot, hotter, frightfully hot; the little Half-Chick cried out, "Do not burn so hot, Fire! You are burning me to death! Stop!"

But the Fire said, "Little Half-Chick, little Half-Chick, when I was in trouble you would not help me," and burned hotter than ever.

Just as the little Half-Chick thought he must suffocate, the Cook took the cover off, to look at the dinner. "Dear me," she said, "this chicken is no good; it is burned to a cinder." And she picked the little Half-Chick up by one leg and threw him out of the window.

In the air he was caught by a breeze and taken up higher than the trees. Round and round he was twirled till he was so dizzy he thought he must perish. "Don't blow me so, Wind," he cried, "let me down!"

"Little Half-Chick," said the Wind, "when I was in trouble you would not help me!" And the Wind blew him straight up to the top of the church steeple, and stuck him there, fast!

There he stands to this day, with his one eye, his one wing, and his one leg. He cannot hoppity-kick any more, but he turns slowly round when the wind blows, and keeps his head towards it, to hear what it says.

Retold by SARA CONE BRYANT

GRANNY BLAKE AND HER WONDERFUL CAKE

Once there was an old woman who baked good cakes to sell. From morning till night her little house was filled with wonderful smells. Chocolate cake and lemon cake and peppermint cake and plum cake. Angel cake and devil's cake and

cinnamon cake and cheesecake. Any kind of cake a body could name, Granny Blake could bake.

All over town, the mothers and fathers ordered cakes from Granny Blake. Birthday cakes for the girls and boys. Welcome cakes for the new neighbours. Wedding cakes for the brides. Even a thank-you cake for the town band. Granny Blake made them all. She never once said no to a single soul.

"Not I," said Granny Blake. "Any cake you want, I'll bake. For I like folks and folks like cake."

Now, with all these orders coming in, you might think that Granny Blake would see lots of folks and eat lots of cake. But no, indeed. What with the measuring and the mixing and the beating and the baking, Granny Blake never had a minute nor a crumb to herself. Not even just before her own birthday, which she didn't once think of.

"Take a day off," said the mothers and fathers when they came for their cakes. "Get someone in to help."

But Granny Blake smiled and shook her head. "Everyone is too busy," she said. And she went right on with her measuring and her mixing.

"Take a week off," said the children when they came to clean out the bowls. "Tell the people 'No'."

But Granny Blake just shook her head. "You'll not hear 'No' from Granny Blake, for I like folks and folks like cake." And she went right on with her beating and her baking as hard as ever.

"This is a fine how-do-you-do!" everybody said. "Too busy to remember her own birthday! Too busy even to make herself a cake!"

All over town they started to whisper. "Do you suppose?" And "Why not?" And finally, "Let's do it!"

"Can you bake us a cake," they said to Granny Blake, "BIG ENOUGH FOR THE WHOLE TOWN?"

"I certainly will," smiled Granny Blake, who never said 'No' to a single soul. "Only how can I ever measure such a great cake? And how shall I ever mix it and beat it and bake it? And wherever shall I put it when it is done? I declare, I do not know!"

But everybody else knew. Because—first, the boys and girls came running with their biggest sand-buckets to help with the measuring. Next, some neighbours brought a big cement-mixer to help with all the mixing and the beating.

Granny Blake and her Wonderful Cake

After that, to help with the baking, each bride popped a different panful of batter into her own oven. Pretty soon the good smells started rising all over town. Chocolate, lemon, peppermint, plum—several of each kind—to please everybody.

As soon as the cakes were baked, the town band fitted them all together on the bandstand, right in the middle of the park. And, last of all, Granny Blake frosted it—the biggest, the yummiest, the most wonderful cake anyone had ever seen!

"There!" said she, as pleased as could be, "Now, what do you want it to say?"

"Happy Birthday," everybody shouted.

"H-A-P-P-Y B-I-R-T-H-D-A-Y," wrote Granny Blake with her decorating tube. "Happy Birthday, who?"

"Happy Birthday to YOU!" everybody sang. "And many happy returns of the day!"

Granny Blake just smiled and smiled. When the candles were lighted, she blew them out, all in one puff. The town band started playing when she opened her presents. They played right through the serving of refreshments, which were gallons of ice cream, barrels of punch and, of course, plate after plate of birthday cake.

They played for a whole week. Because that was exactly how long it took Granny Blake to see everybody and to help eat up her wonderful cake.

Now, would you believe it?

BARBEE OLIVER CARLETON

64

THE TALE OF A TURNIP

Once upon a time there was a little old Man, and a little old Woman his wife, and a little Girl their grandchild, and a little black-and-white Cat, and a little Mouse (that lived where nobody knew but only the little black-and-white Cat): and they all lived together in a little house.

One day the little old Man said to the little old Woman his wife, "I'm going out to the field to plant a seed," and she said, "What kind of a seed?" and he said, "A turnip seed." So the little old Man went out to the field, and he dug a little hole, and he put in a seed (and it *was* a turnip seed), and he went back to the house and said to the little old Woman, "I've planted it!" And they both said, "We hope it will grow."

And it did grow. The sun shone and the wind blew and the rain rained, and a little green shoot came out of the ground, and it grew, and it grew, and it grew, and it *grew* till it grew to a very big turnip (as big as this!). So one day when it was grown (as big as this) the little old Man said to the little old Woman his wife, "Put the pot on the fire and boil some water, and mind it's a big pot, for I'm going to pull up the turnip and we'll all have turnip soup."

So the little old Woman made up the fire and took the biggest pot she had and filled it with water, and put it on the fire to boil the water to make the turnip soup. And the little old Man went out to the field and he caught hold of the turnip, and he pulled, and he pulled, and he pulled, and he *pulled*, but he couldn't pull up the turnip.

So the little old Man called to the little old Woman his wife, "Come and take hold of me, that we may pull up the turnip."

So the little old Woman his wife left the pot boiling on the fire, and she came running out of the house; and the little old Woman his wife had hold of the little old Man her husband, and the little old Man her husband had hold of the turnip; and they pulled, and they pulled, and they pulled, and they *pulled*, but they couldn't pull up the turnip.

So the little old Woman his wife called to the little Girl their grandchild and said, "Come and take hold of me, that we may pull up the turnip."

The Tale of a Turnip

So the little Girl their grandchild came running out of the house; and the little Girl the grandchild had hold of the little old Woman the grandmother, and the little old Woman the grandmother had hold of the little old Man her husband, and the little old Man her husband had hold of the turnip; and they pulled, and they pulled, and they pulled, and they *pulled*, but they couldn't pull up the turnip.

So the little Girl the grandchild called to the little black-and-white Cat, and said, "Come and take hold of me, that we may pull up the turnip."

So the little black-and-white Cat came running out of the house (with its tail in the air, as little cats do when they're pleased); and the little black-and-white Cat had hold of the Girl the grandchild, and the little Girl the grandchild had hold of the little old Woman the grandmother, and the little old Woman the grandmother had hold of the little old Man her husband, and the little old Man her husband had hold of the turnip; and they pulled, and they pulled, and they pulled, and they *pulled*, but they couldn't pull up the turnip.

So the little black-and-white Cat called to the little Mouse (that lived where nobody knew but only the little black-and-white Cat) and said, "Come and take hold of me, that we may pull up the turnip."

So the little Mouse *popped* out of its hole (that nobody knew but only the little black-and-white Cat); and the little Mouse had hold of the little black-and-white Cat, the little black-and-white Cat had hold of the little Girl the grandchild, and

the little Girl the grandchild had hold of the little old Woman the grandmother, and the little old Woman the grandmother had hold of the little old Man her husband, and the little old Man her husband had hold of the turnip; and they pulled, and they pulled, and they pulled, and they pulled, and *up* came the turnip! But the little old Man fell over on top of the little old Woman his wife, and the little old Woman his wife fell over on top of the little Girl the grandchild, and the little Girl the grandchild fell over on top of the little black-and-white Cat, and the little black-and-white Cat fell over on top of the little Mouse (that lived where nobody knew but only the little black-and-white Cat), and on top of them all was the turnip!

But nobody was hurt, and it was a very good turnip, and it made very good soup. There was enough for the little old Man, and the little old Woman his wife, and the little Girl the grandchild, and the little black-and-white Cat, *and* the little Mouse (that lived where nobody knew but only the little black-and-white Cat)—and there was enough left over for the person who told the story!

Elizabeth Clark

THE HARE AND THE HEDGEHOG

Early one Sunday morning, when the cowslips or paigles were showing their first honey-sweet buds in the meadows and the broom was in bloom, a hedgehog came to his little door to look out at the weather. He stood with arms a-kimbo,

whistling a tune to himself—a tune no better and no worse than the tunes hedgehogs usually whistle to themselves on fine Sunday mornings. And as he whistled, the notion came into his head that, before turning in and while his wife was washing the children he might take a little walk into the fields and see how his young nettles were getting on. For there was a tasty beetle that lived among the nettles; and no nettles—no beetles.

Off he went, taking his own little private path into the field. And as he came stepping along around a bush of blackthorn, its blossoming now over and its leaves showing green, he met a hare; and the hare had come out to look at his spring cabbages.

The hedgehog smiled and bade him a polite "Good morning". But the hare, who felt himself a particularly fine sleek gentleman in this Sunday sunshine, merely sneered at his greeting.

"And how is it," he said, "*you* happen to be out so early?"

"I am taking a walk, sir," said the hedgehog.

"A walk!" sniffed the hare. "I should have thought you might use those bandy little legs of yours to far better purpose."

This angered the hedgehog, for as his legs were crooked by nature, he couldn't bear to have bad made worse by any talk about them.

"You seem to suppose, sir," he said, bristling all over, "that you can do more with your legs than I can with mine."

"Well, perhaps," said the hare, airily.

"See here, then," said the hedgehog, his beady eyes fixed on the hare, "I say you *can't*. Start fair, and I'd beat you nowt to ninepence. Ay, every time."

"A race, my dear Master Hedgehog!" said the hare, laying back his whiskers. "You must be beside yourself. It's *childish*. But still, what will you wager?"

"I'll lay a Golden Guinea to a Bottle of Brandy," said the hedgehog.

"Done!" said the hare. "Shake hands on it, and we'll start at once."

"Ay, but not quite so fast," said the hedgehog. "I have had no breakfast yet. But if you will be here in half an hour's time, so will I."

The hare agreed, and at once took a little frisky practice along the dewy green border of the field, while the hedgehog went shuffling home.

"He thinks a mighty deal of himself," thought the hedgehog on his way. "But we shall see what we *shall* see." When he reached home he bustled in and looking solemnly at his wife said:

"My dear, I have need of you. In all haste. Leave everything and follow me at once into the fields."

"Why, what's going on?" says she.

"Why," said her husband, "I have bet the hare a guinea to a Bottle of Brandy that I'll beat him in a race, and you must come and see it."

"Heavens! husband," Mrs Hedgehog cried, "are you daft? Are you gone crazy? You! Run a race with a hare!"

"Hold your tongue, woman," said the hedgehog. "There are things simple brains cannot understand. Leave all this fussing and titivating. The children can dry themselves; and you come along at once with me." So they went together.

"Now," said the hedgehog, when they reached the ploughed field beyond the field which was sprouting with young green wheat, "listen to me, my dear. This is where the race is going to be. The hare is over there at the other end of the field. I am going to arrange that he shall start in that deep furrow, and I shall start in this. But as soon as I have scrambled along a few inches and he can't see me, I shall turn back. And what *you*, my dear, must do is this: When he comes out of his furrow *there*, you must be sitting puffing like a porpoise *here*. And when you see him, you will say, 'Ahah! so you've come at last?' Do you follow me, my dear?" At first Mrs Hedgehog was a little nervous, but she smiled at her husband's cunning, and gladly agreed to do what he said.

The hedgehog then went back to where he had promised to meet the hare, and said, "Here I am, you see; and very much the better, sir, for a good breakfast."

"How shall we run," simpered the hare scornfully, "down or over; sideways, longways; three legs or altogether? It's all one to me."

"Well, to be honest with you," said the hedgehog, "let me say this. I have now and then watched you taking a gambol and disporting yourself with your friends in the evening, and a pretty runner you are. But you never keep straight. You all go round and round, and round and round, scampering now this way, now that and chasing one another's scuts as if you were crazy. And as often as not you run uphill! But you can't run *races* like that. You must keep straight; you must begin in one place, go steadily on, and end in another."

"I could have told you that," said the hare angrily.

"Very well then," said the hedgehog. "You shall keep to that furrow, and I'll keep to this."

And the hare, being a good deal quicker on his feet than he was in his wits, agreed.

"*One, Two! Three!—and AWAY!*" he shouted, and off he went like a little whirlwind up the field. But the hedgehog, after scuttling along a few paces, turned back and stayed quietly where he was.

When the hare came out of his furrow at the upper end of the field, the hedgehog's wife sat panting there as if she would never be able to recover her breath, and at sight of him she sighed out, "Ahah! sir, so you've come at last?"

The hare was utterly shocked. His ears trembled. His eyes bulged in his head. "You've run it! You've run it!" he cried in astonishment. For she being so exactly like her husband, he never for a moment doubted that her husband she actually was.

"Ay," said she, "but I was afraid you had gone lame."

"Lame!" said the hare, "lame! But there, what's one furrow? 'Every time' was what you said. We'll try again."

Away once more he went, and he had never run faster. Yet when he came out of his furrow at the bottom of the field, there was the hedgehog! And the hedgehog laughed, and said: "Ahah! So here you are again! At last!" At this the hare could hardly speak for rage.

"Not enough! not enough!" he said. "Three for luck! Again, again!"

"As often as you please, my dear friend," said the hedgehog. "It's the long run that really counts."

Again, and again, and yet again the hare raced up and down the long furrow of the field, and every time he reached the top, and every time he reached the bottom, there was the hedgehog, as he thought, with his mocking, "Ahah! So here you are again! At last!"

But at length the hare could run no more. He lay panting and speechless; he was dead beat. Stretched out there, limp on the grass, his fur bedraggled, his eyes dim, his legs quaking, it looked as if he might fetch his last breath at any moment.

So Mrs Hedgehog went off to the hare's house to fetch the Bottle of Brandy; and, if it had not been the best brandy, the hare might never have run again.

News of the contest spread far and wide. From that day to this, never has there been a race to compare with it. And lucky it was for the hedgehog he had the good sense to marry a wife like himself, and not a weasel, or a wombat, or a whale!

WALTER DE LA MARE

THE LITTLE GIRL WHO CHANGED HER NAME

Little Caroline Brown was lying in bed. The sun came through the window and shone all over her. But Caroline didn't notice that. She was looking up at the ceiling and saying softly over and over again, "Annette! Annette!"

"Yes—I like it! It's better than 'Caroline'," she said, and she went on again "Annette", first in a high voice, then in a low voice, and then in the kind of voice Mother used when she tucked her in bed for the night.

Suddenly Mother called up the stairs:

"Caroline! Caroline! Time to get up! Betty will be coming for you soon!"

Betty was Caroline's friend.

"Oh, I must tell Mummy and Betty to remember that I'm 'Annette' now—not Caroline," she thought, as she scrambled out of bed.

But it was very difficult, because Mother never could remember in time, and kept saying, "Caroline! *Caroline!*—oh, sorry—Annette."

And as for Betty, she just stared at Caroline and said, "Oh, what a bother! Come on—let's go to the park!"

They walked along the road towards the park gates. Betty said, "Look at that puppy in the window, Caroline."

But Caroline said firmly, "*Not* Caroline—Annette!" and she did not look at the window where the puppy wagged his tail as they passed.

When they reached the park gates, Betty cried:

"Come on, Caroline—I'll race you to the swings!" and she flew across the grass.

Half-way to the swings she stopped. There was no fun in running a race with no one racing with you. And Caroline wasn't running! She was walking slowly, slowly, across the grass. And why did she look so cross?

"Oh, bother!" said Betty to herself. "I've forgotten again! Annette! Annette!" she called loudly, "hurry up, else the swings will be taken!"

At last they arrived at the swings and took their seats. Backwards and forwards they went, higher and higher.

It was lovely swinging there, with the morning sunshine all around and the birds singing in the trees. Betty cried:

"Isn't it lovely, Caroline! I can see almost over the tree-tops! I'm glad we got here first!"

Caroline did not answer.

"Oh, dear!" thought Betty; "why can't I remember?"

A crowd of children came through the park gates and rushed over to the swings. It was *their* turn now, they said.

"It is, really, Caroline," said Betty as she scrambled off; "let's go under the trees and look for birds' nests."

She wandered across the grass, looking up into the trees where the birds called and twittered to one another. Caroline followed slowly. Why *couldn't* Betty remember that her name wasn't 'Caroline' any more?

Suddenly Betty stopped under a tree whose branches hung just above her head.

"I believe there's a nest up there," she whispered loudly; "I'm going to climb up and see."

She crept round the tree-trunk, looking for places where she could put her feet, and then began to climb. Gradually, fitting her toes into the bark of the tree, and pulling with her hands, she climbed higher, until she reached the first branch.

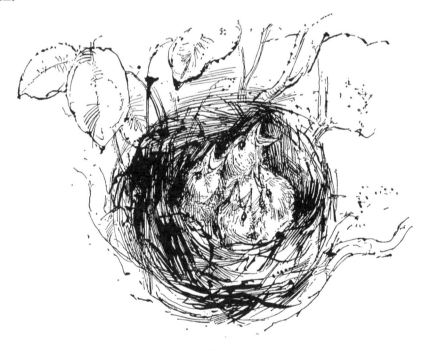

"I do believe I can see it!" she whispered excitedly—"yes, I can! Caroline! Caroline! Come up and see it!"

But Caroline stood by the edge of the trees, and on hearing Betty call, she looked the other way.

"Caroline! Do come and look! There are four baby birds! They're so sweet!"

Caroline did not answer. Her face was sulky and she did not move.

Betty smiled at the baby birds. When they heard a noise they opened their beaks, and then closed them again, all together, like little children doing exercises at school. How soft and fluffy they were!

"Caroline!" she cried, as she climbed down the tree-trunk, "why don't you come and see the baby birds? They're so sweet! Why don't you come?"

Caroline stamped her foot angrily when Betty walked up to her.

"I'm *not* Caroline! I'm Annette! I don't *like* being called Caroline! I think it's a horrid name!"

Betty stood quite still for a minute, and then she began to walk away.

"Where are you going?" cried Caroline.

"I'm going home!" she said firmly. "I *liked* playing with Caroline, but I think this 'Annette' is a *horrid* person. I'm going home!"

And she marched across the grass towards the park gates.

Caroline watched her go. And then she, too, began to walk home, slowly, sulkily. When she arrived at the park gates, Betty was along the street talking to the postman.

"Do you know a little girl named Caroline Brown?" she heard him say.

"No," said Betty sadly, looking back towards Caroline, "her name is 'Annette'."

The postman hurried on his way.

"A letter!" cried Caroline, "a letter! It must be for me!"

She started to run.

"Postman! Postman! I'm Caroline Brown! My name isn't 'Annette'—not really! I was only pretending! Oh, please, *please* don't walk so fast—I shall never catch you! Postman! Oh, please stop!"

Caroline burst into tears.

The postman turned round and stopped.

"What's the matter, little girl?"

"My name isn't 'Annette'—not really," she wept. "I was only pretending. My name's Caroline—truly it is! I liked 'Annette'—better, but if—if you've got a letter for Caroline Brown—it's mine—don't, please, don't take it away—it's mine, really it is!"

75

"Well, well, well!" said the postman; "let's see what we've got?" And he pulled a letter from his bag and read the name out loud, "Miss Caroline Brown."

"Oh!" cried Caroline, "it *is* for me!"

"Well," said the postman, handing her the letter, "there you are! But it's lucky you hadn't forgotten what your *real* name was! For nobody ever heard of 'Annette Brown'!"

IVY M. DUBOIS

THE CROSS SPOTTY CHILD

One day, a long time ago, my naughty little sister wasn't at all a well girl. She was all burny and tickly and tired and sad and spotty and when our nice doctor came to see her he said: "You've got measles, old lady."

"You've got measles," that nice doctor said, "and you will have to stay in bed for a few days."

When my sister heard that she had measles she began to cry: "I don't want measles. Nasty measles," and made herself burnier and ticklier and sadder than ever.

Have you had measles? Have you? If you have you will remember how nasty it is. I am sure that if you did have measles at any time you would be a very good child. You wouldn't fuss and fuss. But my sister did, I'm sorry to say.

She fidgeted and fidgeted and fussed and cried and had to be read to all the time, and wouldn't drink her orange-juice and lost her hanky in the bed until our mother said: "Oh, dear, I don't want you to have measles, I'm sure."

She *was* a cross spotty child.

When our mother had to go out to do her shopping, kind Mrs Cocoa Jones came in to sit with my sister. Mrs Cocoa brought her knitting with her, and sat by my sister's bed and knitted and knitted. Mrs Cocoa was a kind lady and when my little sister moaned and grumbled she said: "There, there, duckie," in a very kind way.

My little sister didn't like Mrs Cocoa saying "There, there, duckie" to her, because she was feeling so cross herself, so she pulled the sheet over her face and said: "Go away, Mrs Cocoa."

But Mrs Cocoa didn't go away, she just went on knitting and knitting until my naughty little sister pulled the sheet down from her face to see what Mrs Cocoa could be doing and whether she had made her cross.

But kind Mrs Cocoa wasn't cross—she was just sorry to see my poor spotty sister, and when she saw my sister looking at her, she said: "Now, I was just thinking. I believe I have the very thing to cheer you up."

My sister was surprised when Mrs Cocoa said this instead of being cross with her for saying "Go away" so she listened hard and forgot to be miserable.

"When I was a little girl," Mrs Cocoa said, "my granny didn't like to see poor not-well children looking miserable so she made a get-better box that she used to lend to all her grandchildren when they were ill."

Mrs Cocoa said: "My granny kept this box on top of her dresser, and when she found anything that she thought might amuse a not-well child she would put it in her box."

Mrs Cocoa said that it was a great treat to borrow the get-better box because although you knew some of the things that would be in it, there was always something fresh.

My little sister stopped being cross and moany while she listened to Mrs Cocoa, because she hadn't heard of a get-better box before.

She said: "What things, Mrs Cocoa? What was in the box?"

"All kinds of things," Mrs Cocoa said.

"Tell me! Tell me!" said my spotty little sister and she began to look cross because she wanted to know so much.

But Mrs Cocoa said: "I won't tell you, for *you can see for yourself.*"

Mrs Cocoa said: "I hadn't thought about it until just this very minute; but do you know, I've got my granny's very own get-better box in my house and I had forgotten all about it! It's up in an old trunk in the spare bedroom. There are a lot of heavy boxes on top of the trunk, but if you are a good girl now, I will ask Mr Cocoa to get them down for me when he comes home from work. I will get the box out of the trunk and bring it in for you to see tomorrow."

Wasn't that a beautiful idea?

Mrs Cocoa Jones said: "I haven't seen that box for years and years, it will be quite a treat to look in it again. I am sure it will be just the thing to lend to a cross little spotty girl with measles, don't you?"

And my naughty little sister thought it *was* just the thing indeed!

So, next morning, as soon as my sister had had some bread and milk and a spoonful of medicine, Mrs Cocoa came upstairs to see her, with her grandmother's get-better box under her arm.

There was a *smiling* spotty child waiting for her today.

The Cross Spotty Child

It was a beautiful-looking box, because Mrs Cocoa's old grandmother had stuck beautiful pieces of wallpaper on the lid and on the sides of the box, and Mrs Cocoa said that the wallpaper on the front was some that had been in her granny's front bedroom, and that on the back had been in her parlour. The paper on the lid had come from her Aunty Kitty's sitting-room; the paper on one side had been in Mrs Cocoa's mother's kitchen, while the paper on the other side which was really lovely, with roses and green dickeybirds, had come from Mrs Cocoa's own bedroom wallpaper when she was a little girl!

My sister was so interested to hear this that she almost forgot about opening the box!

But she did open it, and she found so many things that I can only tell you about some of them.

On top of the box she found a lovely piece of shining stuff folded very tidily, and when she opened it out on her bed she saw that it was covered with round sparkly things that Mrs Cocoa said were called *spangles*. Mrs Cocoa said that it was part of a dress that a real fairy-queen had worn in a real pantomime. She said that a lady who had worked in a theatre had given it to her grandmother long, long ago.

Under the sparkly stuff were boxes and boxes. Tiny boxes with pretty pictures painted on the lids, and in every box a nice little interesting thing. A string of tiny beads, or a little-little dollie, or some shells. In one box was a very little paper fan, and in another there was a little laughing clown's face cut out of paper that Mrs Cocoa's granny had stuck there as a surprise.

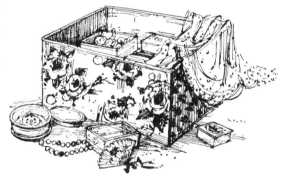

My sister was so surprised that she smiled, and Mrs Cocoa told her that her granny had put that in to make a not-well child be surprised and smile. She said that she remembered smiling at that box when she was a little girl.

Mrs Cocoa's old granny had been very clever, hadn't she?

There were picture postcards in that not-well box, and pretty stones—some sparkly and some with holes in them. There was a small hard fir cone, and pieces of coloured glass that you could hold up before your eyes and look through. There was a silver pencil with a hole in the handle that you could look through too and see a magic picture.

There was a small book with pictures in it—oh, I can't remember what else! It amused and *amused* my sister.

She took all the things out carefully and then she put them all back carefully. She shut the lid and looked at the wallpaper outside all over again.

Then she took the things out again, and looked at them again and played with them and was as interested as could be!

And Mrs Cocoa said: "Well, I never! That's just what I did myself when I was a child!"

When my sister was better she gave the box back to Mrs Cocoa—just as Mrs Cocoa had given the box back to her granny.

Mrs Cocoa Jones laid all the things from the box out in the sunshine in her back garden to air them after the measles. She said her grandmother always did that,

and because Mrs Cocoa's granny had done it, it made it all very specially nice for my little sister to think about.

After that, my sister often played at making a get-better box with a boot-box that Mother gave her, and once she drew red chalk spots on poor Rosy-Primrose's face so that she could have measles and the get-better box to play with.

DOROTHY EDWARDS

THE PRINCESS WHO COULD NOT CRY

There was once a little princess who could not cry.

That wouldn't have mattered so very much, but the trouble was that she laughed at everything, often on the most unsuitable occasions, and this was an extremely vexing and awkward habit, especially for a princess.

Her parents were very troubled about it, and they called in a wise old fairy in order to get her advice. She went into the matter thoroughly, and finally told them that if the princess could only once be made to cry, the spell would be broken for ever and she would thenceforward be just like other people.

This wasn't particularly helpful, but it gave them some hope, and they immediately set about the task of making the princess weep. Of course it was a rather difficult matter, because naturally they didn't want her to be really miserable, and they hardly knew how to begin. Finally they offered a reward of five hundred crowns to anybody who should succeed in making their daughter cry without doing her any harm.

Wise men came from all over the kingdom to see what they could do, and many things were tried, but all to no purpose.

One of them suggested that she should be shut up in a room by herself and fed on bread and water for a whole week. The queen thought this very cruel, but the king persuaded her to try it. She insisted, however, that at any rate it should be bread and *milk*. But every time they came to bring the princess her basin of bread and milk they found her laughing, and at the end of the week she was still as cheerful as ever.

"Look," she said, "my feet have grown so thin that I can't keep my slippers on." And she kicked her foot into the air and sent her slipper flying across the room, and laughed to see the scandalized face of the butler.

But her mother burst into tears. "My poor starved lamb," she said, "they shall not treat you so any longer." And she rushed into the kitchen and ordered soup and chicken and pink jelly to be sent up to the princess for her next meal.

Another wise man came who said that for six months he had been practising pulling the most awful faces and making the most terrible noises imaginable, in

order to be able to cure the princess. Children, he said, were so frightened by him that they had to be carried shrieking and howling from the room, and even grown-up people were so terrified that they wept aloud. He requested that he might be left alone with the princess; but the queen waited outside the door and listened.

She trembled with anxiety as she stood there, for the noises the wise man made were so bloodcurdling that she could hardly bear to hear them herself, and it seemed dreadful that her child should be left alone to endure such a trial. But in a few minutes she heard peals of laughter coming from inside the room, and presently the wise man opened the door. He was quite done up, and blue in the face, with the efforts he had been making. "It's no use," he said rather crossly. "No use at all," and went away looking much annoyed.

The princess came running out to her mother. "Oh, he *was* a funny man," she said. "Can't he come and do it again?"

Another wise man suggested that all her favourite toys should be broken up. But when he went into the nursery and began smashing her beautiful dolls and

playthings, the princess clapped her hands and jumped about and laughed more heartily than ever.

"What fun, what fun," she said, and she too began throwing the things about. So that plan had to be given up also.

Other wise men came, but as many of their suggestions were cruel and unkind ones, naturally the king and queen would not hear of them, and at last they began to fear that nothing could be done.

Now in a small village on the borders of the king's great park, there lived a widow with her little daughter Marigold.

They were very poor, and the mother earned what she could by doing odd jobs of washing, sewing, or cleaning for her neighbours. But she fell ill, and poor Marigold was in great trouble, for she had no money to buy comforts for her mother.

Their little savings had to go for food to keep them alive, and every day these grew less and less.

Marigold knew all about the little princess of the castle. She had often heard of her, and had even seen her sometimes riding about the roads on her white pony. And one day as she was cooking the midday meal an idea came into her head.

As soon as dinner was over, she put on her hat and cloak and told her mother that she was going up to the king's palace to see if she could make the princess cry and so earn the five hundred crowns.

Her mother did her best to persuade her not to go.

"How can you hope to succeed," she said, "when so many clever people have tried and failed? You are my own dear little Marigold, but it is useless for you to attempt such a task. Give it up, my child."

But Marigold was determined, and when her mother saw this she said no more, but lay and watched her rather sadly as she set bravely off for the castle with her little basket over her arm.

When Marigold came to the castle gates she felt frightened. The gates were so big and she was so small. But she thought of her mother and of the five hundred crowns which would buy her everything she needed, and she stood on tiptoe on the top step and pulled the bell handle so hard that she was quite frightened at the noise it made.

A very grand footman opened the door, and when he saw Marigold standing there in her woollen frock and cloak with her little basket, he said, "Back entrance!" in a loud, cross voice, and shut the door in her face.

So she went round to the back entrance. This time the door was opened by a red-faced kitchen-maid. "We've no dripping to give away to-day," she said, and she too was about to shut the door in her face.

But the queen happened to be in the kitchen giving her orders for the day, and she saw Marigold through the window and called to her.

"What is it, my child?" she asked, for Marigold stood there looking the picture of unhappiness.

"I've come to make the princess cry, please your Majesty," she said, and made a curtsey, for the queen looked very magnificent with her crown on her head and her lovely ermine train held up over her arm to keep it off the kitchen floor.

When the queen heard what Marigold had come for, she smiled and shook her head, for how could a little country girl hope to do what so many wise men had been unable to accomplish? But Marigold was so earnest and so sure that she could make the princess cry that at last the queen promised to let her attempt it.

"You won't hurt her?" she said. But she smiled as she said it. Marigold had such a kind little face she did not look as if she could hurt anyone.

She was taken to the princess's apartments, and the queen went with her into the nursery and introduced her to the princess and explained why she had come.

The princess was delighted to see a nice little rosy-cheeked girl instead of the dull old men who so often came to visit her. The queen shut the door and left them alone together.

By this time the news of the little village girl who had come to make the princess cry, had spread all over the palace; and presently a whole crowd of people were standing anxiously waiting outside the nursery door.

"It's such nonsense," said the Chamberlain to the Prime Minister. "A village child. I don't suppose she's ever been outside the village."

"Quite ridiculous," whispered the ladies-in-waiting to the court pages. "Do you think she knows how to make a correct curtsey?"

At last the king and queen could stand the suspense no longer. They quietly opened the door and peeped in. And what do you think they saw? The princess, standing in the middle of the room with Marigold's basket in front of her, busily peeling onions as hard as she could go, while the tears streamed down her face all the while. She was crying at last!

The king and queen rushed in and clasped her in their arms, onions and all. The ladies-in-waiting stood with their perfumed handkerchiefs pressed to their noses, the pages tittered, and the cook, who was standing at the bottom of the stairs, muttered to himself when he heard the news, "Well, *I* could have done that," while the Prime Minister rushed about the room with his wig on one side and shook everybody violently by the hand, exclaiming, "Wonderful, wonderful! And so simple! We must get out a proclamation at once. Where are my spectacles? Where is my pen?"

And so the princess was cured, and from that time she became like everybody else and cried when she was unhappy and laughed when she was glad, though I am pleased to say that she always laughed a great deal more than she cried.

As for Marigold, she got her five hundred crowns, of course, and was able to give her mother everything she needed, so that she was soon quite well. The king and queen were most grateful, and often invited her up to the palace to play with their little daughter, and loaded her with presents.

Because she was sweet and modest she didn't get spoiled, but grew up charming, kind and beautiful. I did hear that in the end she married a king's son and that they had an onion for their crest, but I'm not at all sure about that.

ROSE FYLEMAN

MRS MALLABY'S BIRTHDAY

There was once an old lady who was very, very old. She was so old that she didn't even know herself how old she really was. Her name was Mrs Mallaby, and she lived all alone in a little brick house with a green door, seven windows, and a pretty bright garden growing all around it.

One morning as Mrs Mallaby was finishing her breakfast she heard a knock.

Mrs Mallaby's Birthday

"That's the postman," said Mrs Mallaby. "There must be a letter!" So she hurried to the door.

There was the postman, in his blue coat. "Good morning, Mrs Mallaby," he said. "I believe I have something for you this morning." And he began to hunt through his bag.

"Good morning, Mr Walker," said Mrs Mallaby. "Oh, what will it be?"

"Here it is," said the postman.

Sure enough. There was a little blue envelope with a stamp, and it said: *Mrs Mallaby.*

Mrs Mallaby was much excited. She did not often have any mail. She thanked

Mr Walker, took the letter into the house, and opened it. Inside there was a pretty card with flowers and a ribbon on it and a message that said: *Happy Birthday, Mrs Mallaby! Many Happy Returns of the Day!*

"It must be my birthday!" Mrs Mallaby said.

She put the card up on the mantel and sat down to count. She counted for nearly an hour. Then she said, "I do believe I'm a hundred years old today. My goodness, how time flies! Well, I rather wish I had a kitten."

Just then there was another knock at the door. Mrs Mallaby hurried to open it.

There stood the neighbour who lived next door— Mrs Bowe. She was holding a large package carefully in both hands.

"Many happy returns of the day, Mrs Mallaby!" said Mrs Bowe. "I've brought you a little remembrance for your birthday."

"How very sweet of you," said Mrs Mallaby. "*I hope it's a kitten.*"

She said the last words very low, to herself, so that Mrs Bowe wouldn't know she was disappointed if it wasn't a kitten.

Mrs Bowe set the package on the table and took off the wrappings. Inside was an enormous birthday cake, with one hundred candles on it.

"Oh, thank you, Mrs Bowe!" cried Mrs Mallaby. "How very nice of you!"

Mrs Bowe was pleased. "We'll light the candles," she said, "and then it'll look quite pretty."

So Mrs Mallaby got the matchbox and she and Mrs Bowe lighted the one hundred candles.

"You must have the first piece," she said to Mrs Bowe.

She cut Mrs Bowe quite a large piece of the birthday cake. Then she took a piece herself.

"It's just lovely!" she said. "I've never had such a beautiful cake before."

They sat down and ate their pieces of cake to the last crumb. It was delicious. Then Mrs Bowe said "Good-bye" and "Happy Birthday" and went home.

Then Mrs Mallaby went around her house as she did every day to see that everything was clean and in order.

She washed the dishes and put them away. Then she heard another knock on the door.

She hurried to the door, and who should it be but Dr Blight, another neighbour who lived down the street. Dr Blight was holding a very large, interesting-looking package tightly under one arm.

"How do you do?" he said. "Well, well, well!" (He always said that, even when people were sick.) "I hear you're a hundred! Well, well, well! Many happy returns, Mrs Mallaby, and here's a little birthday present for you!"

Mrs Mallaby ran to get her glasses.

"*Perhaps it will be the kitten this time,*" she said to herself. Inside the wrappings was a handsome green silk umbrella, with a bird for a handle.

"Why, how pretty!" cried Mrs Mallaby. "How did you know just what I wanted to take to church on rainy Sundays! Thank you very much, Doctor. Really, I wanted an umbrella more than anything else *except a kitten.*"

Mrs Mallaby said the last words to herself, very low. She didn't want to hurt the kind doctor's feelings or let him see that she was disappointed.

"You must have a piece of my birthday cake," she said.

So Mrs Mallaby gave the doctor quite a large piece of her birthday cake. And he said, "Well, well, well!" again and "Thank you!" and went away.

"Well, well, well!" said Mrs Mallaby to herself. "If I couldn't have a kitten, of course I would rather have a birthday cake with a hundred candles and a green silk umbrella with a bird for a handle than anything else there is in the world."

She had no sooner said this than there came another rap at the door. There stood Peter, the little boy who lived across the street.

Mrs Mallaby's Birthday

"Happy birthday, Mrs Mallaby!" shouted Peter. He was holding his hands behind him.

"Why, hello, Peter," said Mrs Mallaby. She was greatly pleased. "How in the world did you know it was my birthday?"

"I have a present for you!" cried Peter. He drew it out from behind him. It was a large bundle wrapped in paper.

Mrs Mallaby's heart began to beat very fast. *Perhaps it would be a kitten.*

"Bring it right in," she cried, "and we'll open it."

They put the bundle on the floor. Peter danced about while Mrs Mallaby untied the string. Inside was a big pasteboard box. Mrs Mallaby lifted the cover. There was a beautiful big wooden boat.

"Why, *Peter!*" said Mrs Mallaby. She was so astonished that she could not say another word.

"I made it myself," said Peter. "I made it in school and painted it too. It's for your birthday."

He took it out of the box and held it up for Mrs Mallaby to see.

"It's made out of two blocks of wood. You put one on top of the other and pound them together with nails," he explained. "There are two smoke-stacks— look! And a string to pull it by. I'll come and sail it for you sometimes if you want me to."

"How beautiful it is!" said Mrs Mallaby. "And to think that you made it yourself."

"It wasn't very hard," said Peter.

"I never thought I should have a boat like this," said Mrs Mallaby. "Would you like a piece of my birthday cake, Peter?"

"Yes, thank you," said Peter. "What a lot of candles! On my birthday I had six."

Peter ate a large piece of cake and then said good-bye.

"You don't know where I could get a kitten, do you, Peter?" asked Mrs Mallaby.

"No," said Peter. "I wish I had one myself. Good-bye."

Then there was quite a long while when nobody came.

But just as Mrs Mallaby was watering her geraniums, she heard another rap at the door. She hurried to open it. There on the step stood the postman's wife, looking very smiling. She was holding a package.

"Happy Birthday!" she said. "I've been planning a little present for your birthday, Mrs Mallaby, and here it is. Many happy returns of the day."

"Why, Mrs Walker," Mrs Mallaby said, "how very nice of you!" She looked at the box her neighbour was holding and her eyes grew bright. She felt happy.

"*I do believe it's a . . .*" And Mrs Mallaby stopped just in time, for while she was talking she had untied the ribbon and out of the box tumbled a beautiful hand-made apron.

"Why, dear me!" cried Mrs Mallaby. "What a beautiful apron it is! Blue, with red squares. I am so fond of blue. And I do believe there is a pocket!"

She bent over it hastily to look at the stitches, for she didn't want her good friend Mrs Walker to see the tears in her eyes. But she really did want a kitten more and more. The more she thought about it the more she felt she just *must* have a kitten.

"Won't you have a piece of my birthday cake, Mrs Walker?" she asked. "Mrs Bowe made it for me."

"Oh, thank you," replied Mrs Walker, looking admiringly at the beautiful cake with roses and hills of sugar and green leaves around the edge and what were left of the one hundred candles.

So Mrs Mallaby cut a piece of cake for Mrs Walker, and she went away saying, "Thank you very much," and that she thought it was going to rain later on in the day.

And now it was time for Mrs Mallaby to get her lunch. She decided to have crisp bacon, two fried eggs, corn bread, gingerbread, and tea—and a little blackberry jam. Just as she was about to sit down, what should she hear but another knock at the door! She was quite excited!

And there stood Mr Cobb, the grocer! He had taken off his white coat and put on his Sunday one, which was black and had tails going down behind. And he had on a shiny derby hat. And he was carrying in his hand a little basket, a covered basket, which he was holding high and carefully.

Mrs Mallaby tried hard not to look at the basket, but her heart kept saying, "*It's a kitten basket. If ever I saw a kitten basket in my life that's a kitten basket!*"

Her fingers trembled and she could hardly hear what the grocer was saying.

"Mrs Mallaby," he was saying, "you've been a good cus-tomer to me for many more years than I can remember. Mrs Bowe told me it is your birthday and that you are a hundred years old. When I told that to my wife, she said we must certainly make you a little present." And he lifted the basket and held it out to Mrs Mallaby.

Mrs Mallaby could hardly wait to peer under the cover. When she saw what was there she almost cried. Inside the basket was a neat little package wrapped in white tissue paper and tied with a big silver bow. It couldn't possibly be a kitten!

She turned away so Mr Cobb couldn't see how much she had hoped it would be a kitten.

But Mrs Mallaby was very brave, and she was also very polite (which was why she had so many friends, really) and so she said, "Thank you, Mr Cobb," and, "Won't you have a piece of my birthday cake?"

Then at last she opened the package, and what was inside? Why, a handsome sugar bowl with silver handles and a silver top!

Mrs Mallaby was tremendously surprised. She stared at it and lifted the cover. It was full of lumps of sugar. "It's lovely!" she said. "It was so nice of you and Mrs Cobb to remember me. A sugar bowl—think of it!"

About two o'clock that afternoon, after Mrs Mallaby had finished her lunch and done the dishes and put them away and the kitchen was as clean as a new pin, she sat down by the fire and looked at her presents.

She laid them all out on the table and looked at each one.

There was the pretty birthday card with flowers and a ribbon on it.

There was all that was left of the enormous birthday cake with the one hundred candles, the roses and hills of sugar, and green leaves around the edge.

There was the handsome green silk umbrella with the bird for a handle.

There was the beautiful big wooden boat with two smoke-stacks.

And there was the lovely glass sugar bowl with silver handles and a silver top, and full of lumps of sugar.

"They are very, very nice," said Mrs Mallaby. And because she was such a polite little old lady she would not even let herself think, "*I did want a kitten!*"

Then, because she was really a hundred years old and very sleepy, Mrs Mallaby began to nod a little. She leaned forward in her chair and dozed off into a nap.

It began to rain. The rain beat down steadily against the windows.

And as Mrs Mallaby was dreaming, she heard a little sound:

"M-iaow! M-iaow! M-iaow!"

Mrs Mallaby awoke with a jerk. "What's that?" she said. "Was I dreaming? Have I been asleep?"

She looked all around. There was nothing to be seen and nothing to be heard but the sound of the rain against the windows. Her eyes began to close once more.

Then suddenly she heard it again.

"Mi-a-o-w! Mi-a-o-o-o-w!" very faint and wet and lonesome.

Mrs Mallaby ran to the door and threw it open. There on the doorstep in the rain stood a little black and white kitten. He looked right up at Mrs Mallaby and said, "Mi-a-o-o-o-w! Mi-a-o-o-w! Mi-a-o-o-w!"

"Well, bless your heart," cried Mrs Mallaby. "Did you come on my birthday to live with me?"

And the kitten said, "Mi-a-o-w, Mi-a-o-o-w, Mi-a-o-o-w!" which meant that he had.

So Mrs Mallaby took him into the house and dried him with a clean towel. She ran into the pantry and got a white bowl with roses on it and filled it with milk. The kitten drank all the milk. Then Mrs Mallaby fixed a basket for him to sleep in.

The kitten said, "Mi-a-o-o-w!" and Mrs Mallaby said, "What a beautiful birthday!"

And from that day to this, Mrs Mallaby and the kitten have lived happily together in the little brick house with the green door, seven windows, and a garden all around.

HELEN EARLE GILBERT

THE GREAT HAIRY UNICORN

One morning Mr Hare was hurrying towards the drinking pool. As he skipped through the long grass, he suddenly heard a trembly voice somewhere in front of him call out, "Wh-who g-goes th-there?"

Mr Hare stood still and looked around him. He could see nobody.

"Wh-who g-goes . . . there?" repeated the voice.

"It's me—Mr Hare," he cried. "Who's calling?"

There was a rustle of leaves in the bushes ahead and out stepped the goat. "Th-thank goodness it's only you. It's my turn to act sentinel, and I w-was feeling so n-nervous. It's all right," he called, turning his head, "you can come out. It's only Mr Hare."

From the bushes came Tortoise, Rat, Jackal, Hyena, Antelope and Bushbuck. They glanced around nervously.

"What's the trouble?" asked Hare.

"It—it's L-Lion," cried Rat.

"He's on the r-rampage," joined in Tortoise.

"Says he-he m-must gobble up one jungle animal—every day," cried Antelope.

"Oh, he does, does he?" cried Mr Hare.

"He's been roaring and bellowing about," put in Hyena, "saying he's not particular who he has, whether it's R-Rat or G-Goat or B-Bushbuck——"

"He said," added Bushbuck, "I'll gobble up anybody, Jackal or Hare or——"

"Did he say HARE?"

"Yes——"

"Hm-m! He did, did he?" exclaimed Mr Hare. "Well, we'll soon make him change his tune——"

"But how?" cried all the animals together. "Lion's stronger than any of us. What can we do?"

"I'm not sure—yet," replied Mr Hare. "Come to the pool with me while I have a drink. Then I'll go home and see if I can think of a Bright Idea. Come to my house tomorrow morning about ten. Lion will be asleep then."

Mr Hare took a drink, then hurried home. He walked up and down the garden, gazing up at the sky and down at the earth—but no Bright Idea came.

He stared at the path, at the grass, at the flower beds and at the vegetables. Then he glanced at the clump of bamboos growing near his front door.

"Those knobbly stalks look a bit like horns," he thought—and suddenly a Bright Idea popped into his head.

He could hardly wait till the other animals visited him next morning. He stood at the gate looking out for them. "Come along!" he called gaily. "Come in!"

"Oh, Hare, have you thought of something clever?" cried the animals eagerly.

Mr Hare laughed. "Look at these bamboos. Don't they look rather like horns?" He cut one down. "I'm going to disguise myself. I'm going to pretend to be some strange animal that Lion has never seen."

"What sort of animal?" squeaked Rat.

"Well what sort of animals are there that none of us have ever seen?"

"A—a griffin?"

"A dragon——?"

"*They* haven't got horns," cried Mr Hare scornfully. "Look at this bamboo stalk. Now if I take my knife and sharpen it—like this. There! What does that look like?"

"Like a—like a long straight horn. But you've only cut one——"

"Ex-*actly*! And what strange animal has only one straight horn?"

"Oh! A unicorn!" cried all the animals together.

"But you're too small for a unicorn," cried Hyena. "Lion would never be taken in——"

"Oh, don't worry. I won't let him see all of me!" cried Mr Hare. "I'm going to crouch in that big cave between here and the drinking pool. I shall stick the bamboo horn on my head and I shall call myself—Let me think. The Great Unicorn Hare. No, that's not good enough. The Hare Unicorn. That's not very good either, I know! The Great Hairy Unicorn!"

"Ha! ha! ha!" cried all the animals. "That's a wonderful name."

Mr Hare chuckled. "I'll shout—Oh, dear, I don't think I could shout loud enough. Perhaps you could all hide behind me in the cave—It's quite big enough—and shout with me?"

Mr Hare was holding the bamboo stick in his paw. "I know!" he cried excitedly. "We'll have a chorus. We'll make a great bellowing noise."

The other animals were standing together on the grass. Mr Hare raised his bamboo stick. "Let's have a rehearsal now. When I lower this, I want you all to bleat or squeak or howl at the top of your voices. Ready? Don't make a sound until I lower the bamboo. . . . Now!"

All the animals opened their mouths and a sound like the scream of twenty demons filled the air.

"Ho! Ho! Ho!" laughed Mr Hare. "That's perfect. That ought to give silly old Lion the fright of his life. If you're at the back of the cave, you'll be able to see my head quite clearly. Don't make a sound unless I lower my head, then all call out as you did just now."

"But what are you going to *do*, Hare?" asked Tortoise.

"Leave that to me," Mr Hare chuckled. "I'll frighten silly old Lion away all right. Meet me at the cave about six o'clock."

Punctually at six the animals assembled. They had hardly arrived, when along came Mr Hare looking very odd indeed. The long pointed bamboo horn stuck up between his ears, and round his shoulders he had draped a big woolly hearthrug.

All the animals went to the back of the cave, and Mr Hare sat near the entrance.

"We must make a great noise," he said, "then Lion will be sure to come galloping along to see what it's all about. Remember, don't make a sound, except when I lower my head—then make as much noise as you can. Ready?"

Mr Hare lowered his head, and behind him the animals let out a great squeaking, bleating and howling. Mr Hare raised his head, and the sound ceased. The third time Mr Hare lowered his head there came an answering roar from the jungle. It was Lion! He came bounding through the trees.

Mr Hare raised his head and there was silence. The lion came to a standstill and stared at the entrance of the cave, where dimly in the shadows he could see a weird shaggy creature crouching, with an enormous horn sprouting from the top of his head.

The amazed expression on Lion's face was so comical, Mr Hare nearly burst out laughing, but instead he shouted "Aha!" in the loudest voice he could manage. "So you have come at last, Lion."

"Wh-what d'you mean?" asked Lion, "and who are you?"

"I am the Great Hairy Unicorn!" shouted Hare, "and I have been lying in this cave a long time, waiting for you. I have eaten one hundred elephants, one hundred leopards, one hundred rhinoceroses and ninety-nine lions. One more lion is needed and I have sworn I won't move until I have eaten that other lion, to make the hundred. At last my luck is in."

Mr Hare lowered his head, and made as if to spring.

Behind him the animals roared out, and Lion backed a few steps—looking *very* nervous.

"What sort of animal is this?" he wondered. "I can't see all of him—just his head and shoulders and that huge horn. Maybe he has terrible claws and a mighty tail as well——"

Mr Hare raised his head. "Come along!" he shouted. "I don't wish to be kept waiting!"

"I . . . I've just remembered something," cried Lion. "Er . . . F-for the p-present, I must return to the j-jungle——"

"Why? Will you come back tomorrow?"

"N-no—n-not tomorrow——"

"The next day?"

"N-no——"

"Well, at least perhaps I shall meet you in the jungle one day next week?"

"N-no—I—I've just remembered that I'm m-moving from the district—I'm off—and I—I'm never coming back again!"

"Wait!" shouted Hare, "before you go, I've something to say to you—in case you *do* decide to come back. All the animals in this area are under my protection—so don't you dare lay a paw on any of them. Promise me you'll never worry Antelope, Rat, Bushbuck, Tortoise, Jackal, Hyena—or Hare."

"I w-won't," cried Lion, "I promise."

"Swear by your paws and your tail and your mane!" shouted Hare, "or—I'll spring out on top of you——"

"I—I s-swear by my p-paws and my t-tail and my m-mane."

"Very well. Now you may go." Mr Hare lowered his head, and as Lion

galloped off as fast as his legs would carry him, a joyful squeaking, roaring and bleating came from the back of the cave.

Mr Hare flung the woolly hearthrug from his shoulders.

"Ho! Ho! Ho!" he laughed. "He's gone all right. You can come out now. I only wish you could have seen the expression on Lion's face when he caught sight of me. We won't be troubled by him for a long time."

"Oh, Hare!" cried all the animals, "thank you a thousand times. You were clever! You hoodwinked Lion all right!"

Mr Hare looked very pleased.

"If ever he comes back," he said, "just mention—quite casually—that you've been talking to the Great Hairy Unicorn. That'll keep silly old Lion in his place. But come on! Let's go to the drinking pool. I'm thirsty. It was jolly hot with that hearthrug round my shoulders!"

He skipped over to the jungle path, joyfully followed by all the other animals.

MURIEL HOLLAND

HOW THE POLAR BEAR BECAME

When the animals had been on earth for some time they grew tired of admiring the trees, the flowers, and the sun. They began to admire each other. Every animal was eager to be admired, and spent a part of each day making itself look more beautiful.

Soon they began to hold beauty contests.

Sometimes Tiger won the prize, sometimes Eagle, and sometimes Ladybird. Every animal tried hard.

One animal in particular won the prize almost every time. This was Polar Bear.

Polar Bear was white. Not quite snowy white, but much whiter than any of the other creatures. Everyone admired her. In secret, too, everyone was envious of her. But however much they wished that she wasn't quite so beautiful, they couldn't help giving her the prize.

"Polar Bear," they said, "with your white fur, you are almost too beautiful."

All this went to Polar Bear's head. In fact, she became vain. She was always washing and polishing her fur, trying to make it still whiter. After a while she

was winning the prize every time. The only times any other creature got a chance to win was when it rained. On those days Polar Bear would say:

"I shall not go out in the wet. The other creatures will be muddy, and my white fur may get splashed."

Then, perhaps, Frog or Duck would win for a change.

She had a crowd of young admirers who were always hanging around her cave. They were mainly Seals, all very giddy. Whenever she came out they made a loud shrieking roar:

"Ooooooh! How beautiful she is!"

Before long, her white fur was more important to Polar Bear than anything. Whenever a single speck of dust landed on the tip of one hair of it—she was furious.

"How can I be expected to keep beautiful in this country!" she cried then. "None of you have ever seen me at my best, because of the dirt here. I am really much whiter than any of you have ever seen me. I think I shall have to go into another country. A country where there is none of this dust. Which country would be best?"

She used to talk in this way because then the Seals would cry:

"Oh, please don't leave us. Please don't take your beauty away from us. We will do anything for you."

And she loved to hear this.

Soon animals were coming from all over the world to look at her. They stared and stared as Polar Bear stretched out on her rock in the sun. Then they went off home and tried to make themselves look like her. But it was no use. They were all the wrong colour. They were black, or brown, or yellow, or ginger, or fawn, or speckled, but not one of them was white. Soon most of them gave up trying to look beautiful. But they still came every day to gaze enviously at Polar Bear. Some brought picnics. They sat in a vast crowd among the trees in front of her cave.

"Just look at her," said Mother Hippo to her children. "Now see that you grow up like that."

But nothing pleased Polar Bear.

"The dust these crowds raise!" she sighed. "Why can't I ever get away from them? If only there were some spotless, shining country, all for me. . . ."

Now pretty well all the creatures were tired of her being so much more admired than they were. But one creature more so than the rest. He was Peregrine Falcon.

He was a beautiful bird, all right. But he was not white. Time and again, in the beauty contests he was runner-up to Polar Bear.

"If it were not for her," he raged to himself, "I should be first every time."

He thought and thought for a plan to get rid of her. How? How? How? At last he had it.

One day he went up to Polar Bear.

Now Peregrine Falcon had been to every country in the world. He was a great traveller, as all the creatures well knew.

"I know a country," he said to Polar Bear, "which is so clean it is even whiter

99

than you are. Yes, yes, I know, you are beautifully white, but this country is even whiter. The rocks are clean glass and the earth is frozen ice-cream. There is no dirt there, no dust, no mud. You would become whiter than ever in that country. And no one lives there. You could be queen of it."

Polar Bear tried to hide her excitement.

"I could be queen of it, you say?" she cried. "This country sounds made for me. No crowds, no dirt? And the rocks, you say, are glass?"

"The rocks," said Peregrine Falcon, "are mirrors."

"Wonderful!" cried Polar Bear.

"And the rain," he said, "is white face powder."

"Better than ever!" she cried. "How quickly can I be there, away from all these staring crowds and all this dirt?"

"I am going to another country," she told the other animals. "It is too dirty here to live."

Peregrine Falcon hired Whale to carry his passenger. He sat on Whale's forehead, calling out the directions. Polar Bear sat on the shoulder, gazing at the sea. The Seals, who had begged to go with her, sat on the tail.

After some days, they came to the North Pole, where it is all snow and ice.

"Here you are," cried Peregrine Falcon. "Everything just as I said. No crowds, no dirt, nothing but beautiful clean whiteness."

"And the rocks actually are mirrors!" cried Polar Bear, and she ran to the nearest iceberg to repair her beauty after the long trip.

Every day now, she sat on one iceberg or another, making herself beautiful in the mirror of the ice. Always, near her, sat the Seals. Her fur became whiter and

whiter in this new clean country. And as it became whiter, the Seals praised her beauty more and more. When she herself saw the improvement in her looks she said:

"I shall never go back to that dirty old country again."

And there she is still, with all her admirers around her.

Peregrine Falcon flew back to the other creatures and told them that Polar Bear had gone for ever. They were all glad, and set about making themselves beautiful at once. Every single one was saying to himself:

"Now that Polar Bear is out of the way, perhaps I shall have a chance of the prize at the beauty contest."

And Peregrine Falcon was saying to himself:

"Surely, now, I am the most beautiful of all creatures."

But that first contest was won by Little Brown Mouse for her pink feet.

TED HUGHES

THE THREE BILLY-GOATS GRUFF

Once upon a time there were three billy-goats—Little Billy-Goat Gruff, Middle Billy-Goat Gruff and Big Billy-Goat Gruff.

One day the three billy-goats wanted to cross a river to go to a hillside where the grass was long and green and good to eat. But they could only cross at the bridge and under the bridge was a great big ugly Troll. This Troll had eyes as big as saucers, teeth as sharp as knives and a nose as long as a poker.

Little Billy-Goat Gruff got to the bridge first and began to go across—TRIP TRAP.

"Who's that crossing my bridge?" roared the Troll.

"It's only Little Billy-Goat Gruff. I'm going to the hillside to eat the long green grass and grow fat," said the billy-goat in a small voice.

"Oh, no, you're not! I am coming to gobble you up!" roared the Troll.

"Don't eat me, I'm too tiny and thin. Wait for my brother, he's coming along and he's much bigger and fatter than I am," said the smallest billy-goat.

"All right, be off," said the Troll.

Presently Middle Billy-Goat Gruff came to the bridge and began to go across— TRIP TRAP, TRIP TRAP.

"Who's that crossing my bridge?" roared the Troll.

"It's only Middle Billy-Goat Gruff. I'm going to the hillside to eat the long green grass and grow fat," said the billy-goat in a middle-sized voice.

"Oh, no, you're not! I am coming to gobble you up!" roared the Troll.

"Don't eat me. I'm only half-grown. Wait for my brother, he's coming along and he's much bigger and fatter than I am," said the middle billy-goat.

"All right, be off," said the Troll.

Presently Big Billy-Goat Gruff came to the bridge and began to go across— TRIP TRAP, TRIP TRAP, TRIP TRAP.

"Who's that crossing my bridge?" roared the Troll.

"It's BIG BILLY-GOAT GRUFF. I'm going to the hillside to eat the long green grass and grow fat," said the billy-goat in a great big voice.

"Oh, no, you're not! I am coming to gobble you up!" roared the Troll.

"Oh, yes, I am!" answered Big Billy-Goat Gruff, and he ran at the Troll and caught him on his big strong horns and tossed him high into the air. The Troll

came down SPLASH in the river and the third billy-goat crossed the bridge and went to join his two brothers on the hillside. And the three of them ate and ate the long green grass and grew fat.

Retold by BARBARA IRESON

The pedlar with his caps (see over).

MONKEY TRICKS

Once there was a pedlar who sold caps; grey caps, brown caps, blue caps and red caps. He wore all his caps on his head one on top of the other. First he wore his own striped cap, then five grey caps, on top of these five brown caps, on top of these five blue caps and, right on the very top, five red caps.

One day the pedlar was tired and miserable. He had tried hard all the morning but he had not sold a single cap; not a grey cap, not a brown cap, not a blue cap, not a red cap. So he left the village that did not want his caps and walked slowly on his way.

Outside the village he sat down very carefully under a big tree. He took his caps off and counted them. They were all there, twenty-one caps; his own striped

cap, the grey caps, the brown caps, the blue caps and the red caps. Not one had been sold and he had no money for his dinner. "Still," he thought, as he put them back on his head, "I shall sell some this afternoon." Then he fell fast asleep.

He woke up feeling much better and put up his hand to feel if his caps were safe, but there was only one there. He pulled it off and saw it was his own striped cap. The pedlar was very upset. Up he jumped and looked behind him, in front of him and to both sides. Not a grey cap, a brown cap, a blue cap, or a red cap was to be seen.

Then he looked up in the tree and there were his caps, all twenty of them on the heads of twenty monkeys.

"You thieving monkeys!" he called out. "Give me back my caps." The monkeys said nothing.

"You nasty thieving monkeys!" he cried. The monkeys just stared at him.

The pedlar shook his fist at the monkeys and shouted: "Did you hear me? Give me back my caps." All the monkeys shook their fists at the pedlar, but they did not give him back his caps.

He stamped his foot and shouted: "Don't you shake your fists at me, you ugly little beggars." And the monkeys all lifted their monkey feet and stamped back at him.

The pedlar thought of all the dinners he wasn't going to get because the monkeys had stolen all his grey caps, all his brown caps, all his blue caps and all his red caps. He took off his striped cap and flung it on the ground. "Here," he yelled, "you might as well have this one too."

"Thieving animals!" he called as he went away, and looking back he saw something that made him stop.

Each monkey had taken off its cap and had flung it on the ground. All his grey caps, all his brown caps, all his blue caps, all his red caps lay on the ground. The pedlar ran and picked up every one and put them back on his head; first the grey caps, then the brown caps, then the blue caps, then the red caps. And he walked off whistling towards the next village to sell his caps and buy his dinner.

Retold by JANE ELIZABETH IRESON

HANS AND THE BEAR

Hans lived in Denmark in a little cottage near the woods. He was very poor and he used wood from the forest to keep himself warm. If he had any to spare, he would sell it in the market town and buy himself food with the money.

One day when he was in the town selling wood, he heard the town crier ringing his bell and calling out: "Oyez! Oyez! Oyez!" Everybody stopped buying and gathered round the town crier to hear the news.

"Oyez! Oyez! Oyez!" said the town crier, "His Majesty the King of Denmark desires a volunteer to take a gift to the King of Norway. The reward will be a bag of gold. Interviews will be held at the Palace at 9 o'clock tomorrow. Oyez! Oyez! Oyez!"

Hans pricked up his ears. A bag of gold. That was just what he needed, then he would not have to sell wood in the market again.

Early next morning he presented himself at the Palace only to find many more there before him. However, when the King arrived and told them that the gift was a bear, a white bear, everybody except Hans very quickly disappeared.

"Ah!" said the King. "As you appear to be the only brave man we have around here, you shall have the honour of taking the white bear to my friend, the King of Norway."

Hans was not so sure he was very brave, but he did want the money so he said that he would take the bear. A chain was put round the bear's neck and Hans led it away.

The villagers ran away when they saw Hans leading the bear down the street but Hans started to whistle to give himself courage. The bear must have liked the whistling for he trotted very quietly after Hans and did not give him any trouble.

At the end of the day Hans found a mountain hut where they could stay for the night. He gave the bear some meat which a thoughtful servant had pushed into his hands before he left the Palace, while he had a slice of bread and cheese which he found in his pocket. The bear finished his supper very quickly and soon curled up and went to sleep. Hans was tired out by the long walk and it was not long before he too fell asleep.

The next morning the bear trotted by Hans' side and when they came to a stream they both refreshed themselves with water. They walked all day and by nightfall they had come to the great forest of Norway. Hans had no food left so he stopped at the first log cabin he came to and asked if he could stay for the night. The woodcutter and his wife who came to the door were startled to see the bear, but thought he must be safe if he had travelled with this man all day.

They brought some food from a cupboard and gave Hans and the bear a good meal. "We cannot spare a lot of food," said the woodcutter, "because tonight is the last night of the year and this is the night when the Trolls come to visit. If we do not leave them plenty of food they will wreck our house and rob us of all we

have." Hans wanted to know more about this and the woodcutter's wife said: "We always sleep in the wood shed at the back of the house. They would harm us if we got in their way but you can join us in the wood shed if you like."

Hans thanked them and said he would sleep in the wood shed but he would have to leave the bear in the house as the shed would be too small for them all.

During the night Hans woke up shivering with cold so he went back to the house and shut himself up in a cupboard. The white bear was curled up in front of the fire fast asleep. Just after midnight when the clock had finished striking, there was a loud bang and the door flew open. Hans woke with a start and through a crack in the cupboard door he saw the strangest sight he had ever seen.

In through the windows, in through the door, came the funniest men Hans had ever set eyes on. They were very tiny, like dwarfs, and some had beards and some had whiskers. Blue caps, red caps, black coats, white coats, brown shoes, green shoes, all the colours of the rainbow came pouring into the house. Over the chairs, under the chairs, over the table, under the table, round and round the room scrambled dozens of tiny Trolls. They jumped on to the chairs and on to the table and ate all the food that the old man and woman had left for them. They

looked round to see what else they could find to eat when suddenly one of them saw the bear.

At first they were a little afraid but one bold Troll went up to see what it was. "Why it's a big cat," he said, and all the Trolls gathered round the bear. One prodded him, another tickled him, one pulled his hair and another got hold of his tail and started shouting, "Pussy-pussy, what a big pussy you are!" This woke up the big white bear and turning over he growled at the top of his voice. My what a scramble there was! All the Trolls shouted and yelled and fled for their lives. Under the table, over the table, under the chairs, over the chairs, round and round the room, out of the windows and out of the door, through the woods and back to the mountains they went.

Hans and his bear soon settled back to sleep and did not wake up again until daybreak.

The woodcutter and his wife came in for breakfast and Hans told them what had happened. They laughed until their sides ached and thanked Hans for bringing his bear and frightening the Trolls away.

Hans left them after breakfast and continued on his way. He came to the King of Norway's castle and safely delivered the white bear and the King's message.

The King of Norway was so pleased with the gift that he gave Hans a bag of silver to take back. With this silver and the bag of gold which he received when he got back to Denmark, Hans was very rich indeed and did not have to work very hard again.

The woodcutter and his wife were pleased too because they never saw the Trolls again.

Retold by VERA JACQUES

TEDDY'S OLD COAT

Teddy had an old grey coat that he wore for years and years and years. Through Spring, Summer, Autumn and Winter, he wore it. In rain, in snow, in sleet and sunshine he wore that old grey coat of his. He was very fond of it. When the left elbow of his sleeve began to wear through, he just couldn't throw the old coat away. He decided to patch it. He found he had no grey cloth, so he patched it with a green piece instead. His friends were rather amused to see him trotting around town in his grey coat with a bright green patch on his left elbow. Some poked fun at him in a sly sort of way, but nothing could stop Teddy wearing that old coat of his. Oh, he wore it and he wore it—till one day he noticed that the *right* sleeve was showing a hole at the elbow. But would he throw the old coat away? Never! He had no green cloth left, so he patched it this time with a bit of red. And pretty soon after that his collar began to fray. He had no red cloth left, so he patched it with a bit of purple.

One day he was leaning on a wooden fence talking to his friends, and a sharp nail sticking out of the wood caught in the back of the coat, and ripped it.

"Rrrrrrrip!" it went.

"Oh, Teddy!" cried some of his friends, "now you'll *have* to throw that old coat of yours away!"

"Yes," he said, very mournfully taking off the coat and looking at the great tear in the back, "now I shall have to throw it away, because I've no more cloth to patch it with. But I must say, I don't *want* to throw it away."

"Well," said his good friend, Kangar, "I have a piece of yellow cloth you may have."

Teddy's Old Coat

"Thank you," said Teddy very gratefully.

"Don't mention it," replied Kangar. "As a matter of fact, my dear Teddy, I *like* to see you trotting around town in your old grey coat."

"Yes, Teddy," nodded the others very seriously, "we've got used to seeing you in your old grey coat with its green patch on the left sleeve, the red patch on the right sleeve, and the purple patch on the collar." So saying, they helped him on with his coat. Then they went along to Kangar's house and Teddy took the yellow cloth from him. He made a little speech of thanks. "My very dear friends," he said, and everyone cheered and clapped.

Later on in the evening he was seen trotting around town in his old grey coat with its green patch on the left sleeve, the red patch on the right sleeve, and purple patch on the collar, and a brand new yellow patch across the back. Oh, yes, everyone could recognize Teddy from far off. He continued wearing it right through that autumn, and through the winter too.

However, one day in springtime, Teddy looked at his old coat in the mirror, and began to think that he'd worn it long enough. He suddenly felt that he would like to buy himself a new coat. He didn't know yet what he was going to do with his old one. He took it off, and as he stood there staring at it, there came a soft knock on the door. He opened it, and found a beggarman, dressed in rags and tatters.

"Pardon me, kind sir," said the beggarman. "Can you spare me a copper?"

"I've no money to give you," replied Teddy, "but you may have this old coat, if you like." He gave him the coat.

The beggarman took it with a few words of thanks. He put it on and walked into town quite pleased with himself. However, when he trotted through the

market square in the old grey coat with its green patch on the left sleeve, the red patch on the right sleeve, the purple patch on the collar, and the yellow patch across the back, everyone who saw him rushed up and stopped him.

"Look, he's stolen Teddy's coat!" they cried. "Robber! Thief!"

In vain the poor fellow tried to tell them the truth. His voice was lost in their angry shouting. They caught and pulled the old coat from him, and sent him running out of town with kicks and cuffs. Then they all took the coat and carried it back to Teddy's house.

When they got there Teddy was just coming out to get measured for his new coat at the tailor's. Of course he was only in his shirt, and they cried to him, "Oh, Teddy, don't worry about the coat the man stole from you! We've got it back from him!"

In vain Teddy tried to tell them he had *given* it to the beggarman. His voice was lost in their cheers and laughter. They caught hold of him in the friendliest way, and, putting the old coat around him, pushed his arms through the sleeves.

"My goodness, Teddy!" they cried. "It's nice to see you in your old coat once more!" Then they chattered merrily about this and that for a while, said "Good-bye!" and left him.

Teddy went back into his house, and looked at himself gloomily in the mirror. "I don't see *why* they like to see me in this ragged old coat," he grumbled. "It's patched in four different places, in four different colours, and it's high time I got myself a new one. I know what I'll do," he decided. "If I can't *give* it away, I'll *throw* it away."

So saying, he stepped out of the house and made for the outskirts of the town. When he saw that no one was about he quickly took off the coat, and threw it into a ditch. Then, very pleased with himself, he began to walk back home. When he reached the market square, of course, everyone noticed he was only in his shirt, and they cried, "Teddy, Teddy! Has someone stolen your coat again?"

"No," he replied, "I lost it."

Of course, they were heart-broken. Teddy said he was very sorry too. Just then a little boy came rushing into the square after Teddy, and gave him back his old coat.

"I found it in a ditch!" he exclaimed, beaming with pride, "And I knew it was Teddy's the moment I saw it!"

"Lucky, Teddy!" they cried. "You've got your old coat back!" And they grabbed hold of him in the friendliest way, put it on his back, and pushed his arms through the sleeves. Then they stood back and admired him.

"Please, Teddy," said the little boy, "may I have a penny for finding your coat?"

"Of course, you may!" everyone cried.

So Teddy had to give the little boy a penny. He had to pat him on the head and say what a nice little boy he was. After a while Teddy said "Good-bye" to everyone, and trotted furiously through the town in his old grey coat with its

green patch on the left sleeve, the red patch on the right sleeve, the purple patch on the collar, and the yellow patch across the back. He swung his arms wildly, and grumbled loudly to himself. Oh, he *was* cross! "I'll get rid of this old coat," he vowed. "And this time I'll make sure *no* one'll find it!"

He made straight for the river. When he got to the bank he took off the coat. He felt its weight. This coat's too light to sink, he thought. So he searched around in the bushes for a couple of rocks. Now as he was looking he suddenly noticed someone lying on the bank about twenty yards down. It was his big, bad neighbour, Sore Bear. Fortunately he was flat on his back, fast asleep.

He doesn't look as if he'll wake up for a long time, thought Teddy. So he carried on searching quietly, and soon found two rocks just the right weight. He put one each into the two pockets of the old coat, and got ready to throw it in. I must drop it right in the middle of the river where the water is deepest, he thought, otherwise some fisherman might hook it up and, of course, he'll bring it straight back to me. So saying, he took hold of one sleeve and began to swing the coat around his head. Faster and faster he swung and when he'd got up a terrific speed he suddenly let go of the sleeve.

But, alas! he let go at the wrong moment, and the whirling coat, weighted by the two rocks, flew straight down the bank, and landed with a great thump on Sore Bear! The big chap got up with a most fearful roar, and Teddy ducked and ran into the bushes before he could see him.

But, of course, he knew very well, as he went home, that Sore Bear would recognize the famous old coat. And, indeed, Sore Bear did. He came right over to Teddy's place without wasting a minute. Poor little Teddy was sitting shivering in his kitchen, trying to eat a bun, when there came a crash! and his old coat came flying through the window, rocks and all. So hard did Sore Bear throw it, it knocked all the crockery off the shelf, bounced off the wall, and landed Teddy an awful crack on the head.

When he recovered, and Sore Bear seemed to have gone, Teddy picked up his old coat with one hand and shook his fist at it with the other. "I'm finished with you!" he cried. He took out the rocks, rushed over to the fireplace where a fierce fire was burning, and threw the coat into the flames. And in a minute or two the old grey coat, with its green patch on the left sleeve, the red patch on the right sleeve, the purple patch on the collar, and the yellow patch across the back, went up in smoke.

"*That's* done it," said Teddy aloud. "Now I'm going out to buy me a new coat."

He stepped out of the house in his shirt only and long before he got to the

tailor's shop everyone rushed up to him. "Teddy! Teddy!" they cried. "Has your old coat been stolen again?"

"No," he replied, as they surrounded him.

"Have you lost it again?"

"No," he replied. "You see, it was like this. It was getting dirty, and I washed it. Then I hung it before the fire to dry. Unfortunately the draught must have blown it down on to the fire, because when I came to look at it, it was burnt down to the last stitch."

Of course they were heart-broken. Some of them wailed, and some of them almost burst into tears.

"Make way for me, please," said Teddy, "I'm going to get a new coat made."

He went off, and they all followed him, wringing their hands, and crying what a sad day it was. Well, eventually they got to the tailor's shop, and everyone followed Teddy up to the counter. "Mr Tailor," he said, "I want you to measure me for a new coat—a brand new coat, please."

"Certainly," replied the tailor, getting out his tape measure. "But may I ask what has happened to your old grey one with its green patch on the left sleeve, the red patch on the right sleeve, the purple patch on the collar and the yellow patch across the back?"

"It got burnt!" everyone cried, in the saddest way imaginable. "Burnt! Burnt!"

"Yes," said Teddy, trying not to show how pleased he was now that the old coat was finished and done with. "I'm sorry, but it fell into the fire by accident this afternoon. I hope you'll be able to make my new coat as quickly as possible."

"Certainly," said the tailor, "I shall deliver it personally to your house on Wednesday morning at the latest."

Now that day was Monday. The next day passed without anything happening. On Wednesday morning, rather late, Teddy was sitting in his front garden reading a book, when he heard the noise of a great many voices. He looked down the road, and coming around the corner he could see a procession approaching his house. Everyone he knew seemed to be there, and at their head was the tailor. As they drew nearer Teddy noticed he was carrying a cardboard box bound by a silver ribbon.

It was the new coat, of course. Teddy got up, and the whole crowd marched through the gate into his garden.

"My friends," said Teddy, "my very dear friends——"

"Give him the box, Mr Tailor!" they cried, and everyone fell silent, as he gave Teddy the cardboard box. Teddy took it with a bow, and put it down on the garden table. He untied the knot of the silver ribbon, took off the lid, put it down, and took out the coat.

"Hurray!" a great cheer went up. "Hurray! Hurray!"

Teddy didn't know *what* to say! Mr Tailor had done a beautiful job. It was certainly a brand-new grey coat. But on the left sleeve there was a green patch, and on the right sleeve there was a red patch; and on the collar there was a purple patch, and, of course, across the back was a beautiful bright yellow patch!

AARON JUDAH

HOW BATH BUN GOT HIS NAME

Bath Bun was the name of a little brown bear who lived at the zoo. You might think that was a very funny name for a bear to have, but when I tell you that he was very, very fond of buns, and the bigger the better, perhaps you will understand.

Every fine day during the summer, he would stand on a rock with his mouth wide open, and try to get people to throw buns to him. He was very clever at catching them, and all the little boys and girls who came to the zoo remembered to take a bun with them for the little bear.

During the winter he stayed inside in his cage and slept most of the time—that is, when he wasn't eating, for he was very fond of his food. It was after one of his long sleeps that his big adventure happened.

He woke up one sunny morning and began to sniff round his cage. Somehow one of the catches on the door had come loose, and the little bear noticed this. Very cleverly he pushed it this way and that until he got the door open, and through it he went into the outside world.

"This is an exciting place," he said, and scampered off down one of the paths to see what he could find.

When the keeper arrived to feed him all *he* found was the empty cage with its door swinging open. He called to the other keepers and soon everybody was looking for the little brown bear.

They looked in among the bushes, because they thought that would be a good place for a bear to hide himself—but he was not there.

They looked in the little wood on the hill, for wild bears often live in woods— but he was not there.

They went higher up to the rocks, for bears like climbing—but he was not there. He didn't seem to be anywhere. Then they heard people shouting down below. They were standing in front of the zoo tea-room, looking at something inside.

"That will be our bear," said his keeper. "The rascal will be after a bun." Off they ran down the hill, and when they got to the tea-room there was the little bear sniffing round the tins, and pausing every now and then to stand up on his hind legs with his mouth open.

While they stood looking through the windows, up drove the baker's van with the bread and cakes for the tea-room.

"Now then," said the keeper to the van man, "if you'll just give me one or two of your buns I'll have him back in his cage in no time at all." He picked up a brown sugary one and threw it at the little bear who caught it in his mouth and ate it up with great enjoyment.

"Come on then, little fellow," coaxed the keeper, and this time he threw the bun just inside the door. When it was eaten up he threw the next one outside the tea-room altogether. Slowly he walked away, with the little bear following him still asking for buns, until he got back to the cage. Then he threw the last bun inside it. Through the door after the bun went the bear and by the time he had eaten it up the door was safely locked behind him.

He had eaten so many buns by this time that he was feeling rather sleepy, so he did not mind very much being back in his cage. Indeed he lay down for another snooze. But this is the story of how he got his name. Don't you think it was rather a good one?

MARGARET LAW

THE FAT GRANDMOTHER

Once upon a time there was a little boy, called Kiriki, who lived underground. He lived with his father and mother, and his sisters and baby brother, and his grandmother. It was a queer place to live, but they had always lived there, and so they didn't think it queer. In front of them was a big lake, and at the back of them rocks went up and up, so smooth and steep that they could not be climbed, and so high that no one had ever seen the top of them. Their house was made of shark skins, and so was the canoe they went fishing in. The ground was sand and stones, and nothing grew there, so they lived on fish and seaweed, and drank the water that dripped from the high, smooth rocks. They had a dog, and he, too, lived on fish and seaweed. They were all rather thin, except the grandmother, who was

The Fat Grandmother

horribly fat; and they were all happy, except the grandmother, who was selfish and greedy, and always complaining.

As soon as she woke in the morning the grandmother roared out, "Where is my BREAKFAST?" And as soon as she had gobbled up her breakfast, she roared out, "Where is my PIPE?" And as soon as she had smoked her pipe, she roared out, "Where is my DINNER?" And as soon as she had gobbled up her dinner, she roared out, "Are we never going to have anything decent to eat? Where is my SUPPER?" She gobbled and gobbled, and got fatter and fatter, till she was shapeless with fat.

In the lake there lived an old turtle, and Old Turtle and little boy Kiriki were great friends. Old Turtle would poke his flat head out of the water and say, "Coming for a ride?" And then Kiriki would swim out and climb on his back, and off they would go over the glimmering waters of the lake. But however far they went, they never came to the end of the lake. Kiriki thought it had no end; and if Old Turtle knew differently, he never said so.

But one day Old Turtle didn't come and poke his head out of the water. And another day he didn't come, and yet another day. He didn't come for such a long time that Kiriki felt sad.

"I think a shark has eaten Old Turtle," he said to his father.

"Old Turtle has a thick shell and knows how to take care of himself," said the father.

But Kiriki was very sad, for all that.

And then one day Old Turtle came back. He did more than poke his head out of the water, he came right out of the lake and ambled on his funny short legs over the sand and stones to Kiriki. Then he opened his funny thin lips in a kind of smile.

"Where have you been?" said Kiriki.

"Never mind," said Old Turtle. "I've brought you a present. Put your fingers under my tongue."

Kiriki put his fingers under Old Turtle's tongue.

"Feel anything?" said Old Turtle.

"Only a tiny pebble sort of a thing," said Kiriki.

"Take it out," said Old Turtle.

So Kiriki took the tiny pebble sort of a thing from under Old Turtle's tongue. It was small and dark and hard. Kiriki held it in his hand and looked at it. It didn't seem much of a present.

"It's very precious," said Old Turtle.

"Is it?" said Kiriki.

"I'll tell you what you must do," said Old Turtle. "You must plant it."

"Plant it?" said Kiriki. "What's that?"

"At the bottom of the rocks," said Old Turtle.

Kiriki didn't understand a bit, but he liked Old Turtle and was willing to please him. So Old Turtle showed him how to plant the little seed, for that's what it was.

121

He planted it in the sand at the bottom of the high, steep rocks, and mixed rotted seaweed with the sand, as Old Turtle told him to do.

"Now," said Old Turtle, "you must pour water on it night and morning, and watch carefully. And by and by you will see what you will see."

Kiriki did as Old Turtle said. He watched carefully; but the next day he didn't see anything, nor on the day after that, nor on the day after. But, on the fourth morning, when he went to the place with a shell full of water, there, sticking up out of the sand, was a thin green spike.

"Something's happened!" shouted Kiriki. "Come and look!"

All the family came running to look, except the grandmother, and she went on gobbling up her breakfast.

What was it? They stared and stared. They had never seen anything like it before.

"What are you all doing over there?" roared the grandmother. "Bring me some MORE BREAKFAST!"

But nobody took any notice of her.

It was a wild vine seed that Kiriki had planted, and the wild vine grew and grew. It shot out leaves, and it shot out branches. It clung to the rocks and it went on growing. It grew as high as Kiriki's head, and then it grew as high as the father's head. And then it grew so high that Kiriki had to crane back his head to see the top of it, and then it grew so high that he couldn't see the top of it at all. Its leaves shone, and its branches twisted and thickened, and its tendrils clung to the smooth rock like fingers. Kiriki was never tired of watching it.

One day when Kiriki stood admiring his vine, Old Turtle came out of the lake and ambled up to him.

"Well?" said Old Turtle.

"It is indeed a splendid present," said Kiriki.

"Then use it, use it!" said Old Turtle.

"Use it—how?" said Kiriki.

"Climb it, climb it!" said Old Turtle.

"Shall I?" said Kiriki.

"It's what it's for," said Old Turtle.

So Kiriki put his feet among the lowest branches and clung with his hands to the branches above, and began to climb.

He climbed and he climbed. He climbed so high that when he looked down he couldn't see his home, and he began to be afraid and thought he had better go back. But he didn't go back, because just then he saw something golden above him, and he thought he must find out what *that* was.

The Fat Grandmother

It was a ray of sunlight that Kiriki had seen, but of course he didn't know that. So he went on climbing till he got to the top, and then he stepped out.

He saw blue sky and white clouds, and green grass and flowers, and little woods and great forests, and rivers flowing, and hills and valleys, and creatures moving about. He went up to one creature and asked its name and it said Deer. And he went up to another and asked its name, and it said Sheep. And another said Fox, and another said Hare. And he went up to a very small creature and asked *its* name, and it said Mouse.

"And what place is this?" asked Kiriki.

"This place?" said Mouse, scratching his ear. "This place? Why, it's The Place Where We Live, of course." And he gave a twitch of his tail, and darted under a fallen log.

Kiriki gaped, and Kiriki stared, and then he clapped his hands and jumped for joy. And then he ran and clambered back down the vine as quickly as ever he could.

The family had just finished dinner, and the fat grandmother was sitting on a stone and shouting, "Am I never going to have anything to eat? Where is my SUPPER?"

"And where have you been all this time, Kiriki?" asked the father.

"Oh, oh!" cried Kiriki. "I've been to The Place Where We Live. Come and see!"

So the father climbed up the vine and stepped out. And he was so excited that he came back down the vine like a streak of light.

"Hurry, hurry!" he said. "We're packing up and leaving here! We're going up the ladder to The Place Where We Live."

So they rolled up their sealskin blankets, and each one took a bundle on his back. The father put his stone axe and his fishing lines into his bundle, and the mother put her bone needle and her sewing thread made of seal-tendon into her bundle. The father took the dog under his arm, and began to climb; the mother took the baby under her arm, and began to climb; the sisters followed, and Kiriki came last. He stood at the foot of the vine, and Old Turtle stood beside him.

"Come along," said Kiriki to Turtle.

"Come along, indeed!" said Old Turtle. "I can't climb. My legs are the wrong shape."

"Then I'll carry you," said Kiriki.

"I daresay you will," said Old Turtle. "And drop me too—no thank you!"

"But I'm not going without you!" said Kiriki.

"Yes, you are," said Old Turtle. "Now don't cry. Some day I'll swim round."

"Swim round?" said Kiriki. "Can you?"

"Can't I?" said Old Turtle. "But it's a long way, so you mustn't worry if you don't see me for some time."

Then Old Turtle ambled down towards the lake again, and Kiriki began to climb up after the others.

The grandmother was sitting on the stone; she was still chewing, and roaring out between the chews, "Where's my SUPPER?"

"Aren't you going?" asked Old Turtle.

The grandmother's mouth was full of grilled salmon.

"I want my SUPPER! Bring me my SUPPER!" she roared.

"I'm sorry I can't do that," said Old Turtle, and he ambled into the lake and swam off.

The grandmother went on roaring, "Where's my SUPPER?" and when nobody answered she got off the stone and looked round. And there she was, all alone. So she waddled heavily to the foot of the vine, and roared up, "I want my SUPPER! Who's going to bring me my SUPPER?"

She could see Kiriki far up the vine, and she took hold of the branches and shook them. "Come down!" she roared. "Come down and get my SUPPER!"

But Kiriki only turned his head and shouted, "Come up!" and his voice sounded very small and far away.

The grandmother saw there was no help for it. There was no one left to cook for her or bring her anything. So she put her fat feet on the lowest branches, and took hold of the branches above with her fat hands, and began to climb. She puffed and groaned and scolded and shouted, but up she went, and up she went, with the branches bending and cracking under her weight.

Kiriki had now got to the top and stepped out with the others, and they were all jumping and shouting for joy in the bright sunlight. And the grandmother climbed on.

"I want my SUPPER! Bring me my SUPPER!" she groaned, for she had no breath left to roar with.

But the higher she went, the slenderer grew the branches, and the more they cracked and bent under her weight. Until—the branch that she had her feet on bent right over, and the branch she was clutching with her hands snapped in two, and down, down, *down* she fell.

She knocked herself silly; but by and by she recovered and sat up. And there was Old Turtle looking at her.

"A pity to be so fat," said Old Turtle.

"Don't be impertinent!" wheezed the grandmother. "Bring me my SUPPER!"

Old Turtle brought her a herring, for he was very good-natured.

"Cook it, stupid!" wheezed the grandmother.

"I'm sorry, I can't do that," said Old Turtle. "I don't know how to."

The grandmother threw the herring at him. Old Turtle caught it and put it back in the lake. Then he swam away. The grandmother shouted after him to come back. But he didn't.

Now she was all alone and had to eat seaweed. And the fire had gone out, so she couldn't light her pipe.

She was in a bad way. She ate quantities of seaweed and some cockles and mussels; but she felt sick with all that cold, raw food, and she got thinner and thinner and lighter and lighter, till at last she was just like other people. And when that day came, she thought she would try climbing again.

So she did; and the vine didn't break, and she got to the top and stepped out, and found the family. They had built themselves a fine house of elm bark, and kept a lot of sheep. They had a birch-bark canoe, too, and went fishing in the rivers. They were quite pleased to see the grandmother, but they were busy; they had got out of the way of doing everything she told them, and didn't see why they should begin again. She had to make herself useful, and so she didn't get any fatter than the rest.

Old Turtle was swimming and swimming. And after a long, long time, he came up one of the rivers into The Place Where We Live, and paid Kiriki a visit, as he had promised.

RUTH MANNING-SANDERS

THE MAGIC HILL

Once upon a time there was a King who had seven children. The first three were boys, and he was glad about this because a King likes to have three sons; but when the next three were sons also, he was not so glad, and he wished that one of them had been a daughter. So the Queen said, "The next shall be a daughter." And it was, and they decided to call her Daffodil.

The Magic Hill

When the Princess Daffodil was a month old, the King and Queen gave a great party in the palace for the christening, and the fairy Mumruffin was invited to be godmother to the little Princess.

"She is a good fairy," said the King to the Queen, "and I hope she will give Daffodil something that will be useful to her. Beauty or Wisdom or Riches or——"

"Or Goodness," said the Queen.

"Or Goodness, as I was about to remark," said the King.

So you will understand how anxious they were when the fairy Mumruffin looked down at the sleeping Princess in her cradle and waved her wand.

"They have called you Daffodil," she said, and then she waved her wand again:

> "*Let Daffodil*
> *The gardens fill.*
> *Wherever you go*
> *Flowers shall grow.*"

There was a moment's silence while the King tried to think this out.

"What was that?" he whispered to the Queen. "I didn't quite get that."

"Wherever she walks flowers are going to grow," said the Queen. "I think it's sweet."

"Oh," said the King. "Was that all? She didn't say anything about——"

"No."

"Oh, well."

He turned to thank the fairy Mumruffin, but she had already flown away.

It was nearly a year later that the Princess first began to walk, and by this time everybody had forgotten about the fairy's promise. So the King was rather surprised, when he came back from hunting one day, to find that his favourite courtyard, where he used to walk when he was thinking, was covered with flowers.

"What does this mean?" he said sternly to the chief gardener.

"I don't know, Your Majesty," said the gardener, scratching his head. "It isn't *my* doing."

"Then who has done it? Who has been here today?"

"Nobody, Your Majesty, except Her Royal Highness, Princess Daffodil, as I've been told, though how she found her way there, such a baby and all, bless her sweet little——"

"That will do," said the King. "You may go."

For now he remembered. This was what the fairy Mumruffin had promised.

That evening the King and Queen talked the matter over very seriously before they went to bed.

"It is quite clear," said the King, "that we cannot let Daffodil run about every-

128

where. That would never do. She must take her walks on the flower beds. She must be carried across all the paths. It will be annoying in a way, but in a way it will be useful. We shall be able to do without most of the gardeners."

"Yes, dear," said the Queen.

So Daffodil as she grew up was only allowed to walk on the beds, and the other children were very jealous of her because they were only allowed to walk on the paths; and they thought what fun it would be if only they were allowed to run about on the beds just once. But Daffodil thought what fun it would be if she could run about the paths like other boys and girls.

One day, when she was about five years old, a court doctor came to see her. And when he had looked at her tongue, he said to the Queen:

"Her Royal Highness needs more exercise. She must run about more. She must climb hills and roll down them. She must hop and skip and jump. In short, Your Majesty, although she is a Princess, she must do what other little girls do."

"Unfortunately," said the Queen, "she is not like other little girls." And she sighed and looked out of the window. And out of the window, at the far end of the garden, she saw a little green hill where no flowers grew. So she turned back to the court doctor and said, "You are right; she must be as other little girls."

So she went to the King, and the King gave the Princess Daffodil the little green hill for her very own. And every day the Princess Daffodil played there, and

flowers grew; and every evening the girls and boys of the countryside came and picked the flowers.

So they called it the Magic Hill. And from that day onward flowers have always grown on the Magic Hill, and boys and girls have laughed and played and picked them.

A. A. MILNE

THE LITTLE RED HEN

There was once a little Red Hen who lived in a house all by herself. Now, over the hill, in a dark den, lived a fox with his old, old mother. This rascal of a fox thought that the little Red Hen would make a good dinner, and he wondered how he could get hold of her. He thought and he thought until he grew so thin there was nothing left of him but skin and bone. But he could not catch the little Red Hen for she was too clever for him.

Every time she went out she locked the door behind her, and every time she went in she locked the door behind her, and put her key in her pocket where she kept her scissors and her piece of sugar candy.

At last the rascal of a fox thought of a way to catch the little Red Hen. Early one morning he said to his old mother, "Have a pot boiling when I come home tonight, for I'll be bringing the little Red Hen home for supper."

Then he slung his bag over his shoulder, and away he went till he came to the little Red Hen's house. The little Red Hen was just coming out of her door to gather firewood. So that rascal of a fox hid behind the woodpile, and as soon as she bent down to pick up the wood, he slipped into the house, and hid behind the door.

When the little Red Hen came in, she shut the door and locked it, and put the key into her pocket with her scissors and sugar candy.

And then she saw that rascal of a fox standing there with his bag slung over his shoulder.

Whuff! What a surprise! She was so scared she dropped her bundle of wood and flew straight up to the beam across the ceiling. There she sat, quite out of breath, and peered down at the fox below.

"You may as well go home," said the little Red Hen, "for you'll not get me up here!"

"Ho! ho! ho!" said the fox. "Can't I though!"

And what do you think he did? He stood on the floor, just under the little Red Hen and whirled and whirled in a circle after his own tail. He whirled, and whirled, and as he whirled faster and faster the poor little Red Hen got so dizzy she had to let go of the beam. Down she fell, and that rascal of a fox just picked her up and popped her into his bag.

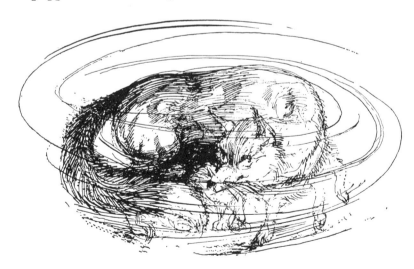

Away he went up the hill, while the little Red Hen was still so dizzy inside the bag she did not know where she was. But as they went on the dizziness wore off, and she began to wonder what she could do to escape the fox. She remembered the scissors in her apron pocket. Snip! She cut a wee hole in the bag, and then she poked her head out to see where she was. As soon as the fox stopped to have a rest, she cut the hole a little bigger and jumped out. A big stone was lying there, so the little Red Hen picked it up and popped it in the bag, quick as a wink. Then she ran as fast as she could till she came to her own wee house. She ran inside and locked the door. Goodness! Was she glad to get home!

Now, that rascal of a fox carried the stone in his bag and never knew the difference. He was pretty tired by the time he reached his den, but he was so pleased with himself, thinking of the fine supper he was going to have, that he did not mind at all.

"Have you got that pot boiling?" he called to his mother.

"Sure I have," said she. "Have you got the little Red Hen?"

"I have," said the fox, "and as soon as I open the bag, you take the lid off the pot so that I can drop her straight in. Then pop the lid back on, before she can jump out."

"I'll do that," said his old mother, and she stood close to the boiling pot, ready.

The fox lifted the bag up till it was over the pot, and gave it a shake. Splash!

Plonk! Splash! In went the stone and out splashed the boiling water, all over that rascal of a fox and his greedy old mother. They were so badly scalded that they never went after hens again.

As for the little Red Hen, she lived happily ever after in her own wee house.

NORAH MONTGOMERIE

JOHNNIKIN AND THE FOX'S TAIL

There was a fox once, and he lived in the middle of a forest, and his tail was the longest tail that ever a fox had.

There was a wee boy called Johnnikin, and he lived at the edge of the forest, and he wanted to ride on the fox's tail more than he wanted to run or skip or play.

One day his grandparents had to go into the forest to chop wood, so they made a nice bowl of soup, and they said to Johnnikin, "Don't let anyone in while we're away, and when we come home you shall ride piggy-back."

Johnnikin waved good-bye and shut the door, but he said, "I don't want to ride piggy-back. I want to ride on the fox's tail."

Well, his grandparents hadn't been gone very long before, scritch-scratch, someone came along the garden path and tapped at the door.

> "*Open, open, Johnnikin,*
> *Open the door and let me in.*"

"I'm not allowed to!" said Johnnikin.

> "*Johnnikin, let me come inside,*
> *And on my tail you shall have a ride!*"

When he heard that, Johnnikin jumped off his chair, opened the door, and there stood the fox, grinning. It walked straight in and, snipper-snapper-lick-a-platter, gobbled up the soup and ran away.

"Dear, dear, what did we tell you?" said Grandpapa and Grandmama when they came home and found Johnnikin crying for his dinner.

Well, next day they had to go out again, so they made a nice bowl of porridge, and said, "Be sure you don't open the door even a crack, and when we come home you shall ride piggy-back."

Johnnikin shut the door. "I don't want to ride piggy-back," he said crossly. "I want to ride on Foxy's tail."

He hadn't been alone very long before, scritch-scratch, someone came along the garden path and tapped at the door.

> "*Johnnikin, let me come inside,*
> *And on my tail you shall have a ride.*"

Johnnikin crept to the door and opened it just a crack. Before he knew where he was, the fox gave it a push with his nose, walked up to the table, and, snipper-snapper-lick-a-platter, gobbled up the porridge and ran away.

"What did we tell you?" said Grandpapa and Grandmama when they came home and found Johnnikin crying for his dinner. "Dear, dear, we shall have to lock the door."

So the next time they had to go out, Granny made a nice pot of stew, and Grandpapa locked the door and put the key in his pocket.

"Be a good boy, Johnnikin," they said, "and you shall ride piggy-back when we come home."

But Johnnikin said, "I don't want to ride piggy-back," and he sat and kicked the legs of his chair.

He hadn't been alone for very long before he heard a polite voice say:

Johnnikin and the Fox's Tail

> "*Open, Johnnikin, open wide,*
>   *And on my tail you shall have a ride.*"

"Go away!" shouted Johnnikin. "You don't keep your promises and the door's locked."

Plop! The fox jumped through the window. Snipper-snapper-lick-a-platter, it was gobbling up the stew, when, plump, down sat Johnnikin on its tail.

"Gee up!"

Out of the window jumped the fox and galloped through the forest.

"Woah!" cried Johnnikin, but the fox went faster.

"Stop!" cried Johnnikin, but the fox went faster still.

Faster, faster, faster, right into the middle of the forest and down its own hole.

And when Grandpapa and Grandmama came home, they found no dinner and no Johnnikin.

"Give me my pipe," said Grandpapa. "I'll play tootle-loo, and fetch him home."

"Give me the iron pot," said Grandmama. "I'll drum rub-a-dub, and fetch him home."

And back they went into the forest till they came to the fox's hole. Then Grandpapa played on his pipe, and Grandmama drummed on her iron pot and sang a song.

> "*Three little foxes live within*
>   *And the fourth is Johnnikin.*
>   *We have a pipe and we have a drum,*
>   *Come and dance, little foxes, come! come! come!*"

"Peep out and see who that is," said the fox to the biggest cub.

The cub hopped out, and Grandpapa caught him and shoo-ed him away out of the forest.

Then Grandpapa began to pipe and Grandmama began to drum.

> *"Two little foxes live within*
> *And the third is Johnnikin.*
> *We have a pipe and we have a drum,*
> *Come and dance, little foxes, come! come! come!"*

"Go out and see who that is and bring your brother back," said the fox to the smaller cub.

The little cub hopped out, and Grandpapa caught him and shoo-ed him away out of the forest.

Then he began to pipe and she began to drum.

> *"One little fox is now within,*
> *Sitting down by Johnnikin.*
> *We have a pipe and we have a drum,*
> *Come and dance, little foxy, come! come! come!"*

"Bother," said the fox. "I must go up and see for myself!"

He jumped out of the hole and "Got you!" cried Grandpapa, and threw him into the pot and clapped on the lid.

Then Grandpapa crept down into the hole, playing his pipe very quietly.

Then Grandmama crept down after him, drumming very slowly, because the pot was heavy with the fox inside it.

And they went down,

And down,

And down,

And down,

And there they found Johnnikin, crying for his Grandpapa and for his Grandmama and for his dinner. So they left the fox to struggle out of the pot all by himself, and took Johnnikin home. And this time Johnnikin wanted to ride piggy-back all the way.

RHODA POWER

TWO OF EVERYTHING

Mr and Mrs Hak-Tak were rather old and rather poor. They had a small house in a village among the mountains and a tiny patch of green land on the mountain side. Here they grew the vegetables which were all they had to live on, and when it was a good season and they did not need to eat up everything as soon as it was grown, Mr Hak-Tak took what they could spare in a basket to the next village which was a little larger than theirs, and sold it for as much as he could get. Then he bought some oil for their lamp, and fresh seeds, and every now and then, but not often, a piece of cotton stuff to make new coats and trousers for himself and his wife. You can imagine they did not often get the chance to eat meat.

Now, it happened one day that when Mr Hak-Tak was digging in his precious patch, he unearthed a big brass pot. He thought it strange that it should have been there for so long without his having come across it before, and he was disappointed to find that it was empty; still he thought they would find some use for it, so when he was ready to go back to the house in the evening he decided to take it with him. It was very big and heavy and, in his struggles to get his arms round it and raise it to a good position for carrying, his purse, which he always took with him in his belt, fell to the ground, and, to be quite sure it was safe, he put it inside the pot and so staggered home with his load.

137

As soon as he got into the house Mrs Hak-Tak hurried from the inner room to meet him.

"My dear husband," she said, "whatever have you got there?"

"For a cooking pot it is too big; for a bath it is too small," said Mr Hak-Tak. "I found it buried in our vegetable patch and so far it has been useful in carrying my purse home for me."

"Alas," said Mrs Hak-Tak, "something smaller would have done as well to hold any money we have or are likely to have," and she stooped over the pot and looked into its dark inside.

As she stooped, her hairpin—for poor Mrs Hak-Tak had only one hairpin for all her hair and it was made of carved bone—fell into the pot. She put in her hand to get it out again, and then she gave a loud cry which brought her husband running to her side.

"What is it?" he asked. "Is there a viper in the pot?"

"Oh, my dear husband," she cried, "what can be the meaning of this? I put my hand into the pot to fetch out my hairpin and your purse, and look, I have brought out two hairpins and two purses, both exactly alike."

"Open the purse. Open both purses," said Mr Hak-Tak. "One of them will certainly be empty."

But not a bit of it. The new purse contained exactly the same number of coins as the old one—for that matter, no one could have said which was the old—and it meant, of course, that the Hak-Taks had exactly twice as much money in the evening as they had had in the morning.

"And two hairpins instead of one!" cried Mrs Hak-Tak, forgetting in her excitement to do up her hair which was streaming over her shoulders. "There is something quite unusual about this pot."

"Let us put in a sack of lentils and see what happens," said Mr Hak-Tak, also becoming excited.

They heaved in the bag of lentils and when they pulled it out again—it was so big it almost filled the pot—they saw another bag of exactly the same size waiting to be pulled out in its turn. So now they had two bags of lentils instead of one.

"Put in the blanket," said Mr Hak-Tak. "We need another blanket for the cold weather." And, sure enough, when the blanket came out, there lay another behind it.

"Put in my wadded coat," said Mr Hak-Tak, "and then when the cold weather comes there will be one for you as well as me. Let us put in everything we have in turn. What a pity we have no meat or tobacco, for it seems the pot cannot make anything without a pattern."

Then Mrs Hak-Tak, who was a woman of great intelligence, said, "My dear husband, let us put in our purse again and again and again. If we take two purses out each time we put one in, we shall have enough money by to-morrow evening to buy everything we lack."

"I'm afraid we may lose it this time," said Mr Hak-Tak, but in the end he agreed, and they dropped in the purse and pulled out two, then they added the new money to the old and popped it in again and pulled out the larger amount twice over. After a while the floor was covered with old leather purses and they decided just to throw the money in by itself. It worked quite as well and saved trouble; every time, twice as much money came out as went in, and every time they added the new coins to the old and threw them in all together. It took them hours to tire of this game, but at last Mrs Hak-Tak said, "My dear husband, there is no need for us to work so hard. We shall see to it that the pot does not run away, and we can always make more money as we want it. Let us tie up what we have."

It made a huge bundle in the extra blanket and the Hak-Taks lay and looked at it for a long time before they slept, and talked of all the things they would buy and the improvements they would make in the cottage.

The next morning they rose early and Mr Hak-Tak filled a wallet with money from the bundle and set off for the village to buy more things in a morning than he had bought in fifty whole years.

Mrs Hak-Tak saw him off and then she tidied up the cottage and put the rice on to boil and had another look at the bundle of money and made herself a whole set of new hairpins from the pot, and about twenty candles instead of one which was all they had possessed up to now. After that she slept for a while, having been up so late the night before, but just before the time when her husband should be back, she awoke and went over to the pot. She dropped in a cabbage leaf to make sure it was still working properly, and when two leaves came out she sat down on the floor and put her arms round it.

"I do not know how you came to us, my dear pot," she said, "but you are the best friend we ever had."

Then she knelt up to look inside it; at that moment her husband came to the door, and, turning quickly to see all the wonderful things he had brought, she overbalanced and fell into the pot.

Mr Hak-Tak put down his bundles and ran across and caught her by the ankles and pulled her out, but, Oh, mercy, no sooner had he set her carefully on the floor than he saw the kicking legs of another Mrs Hak-Tak in the pot! What was he to do? Well, he could not leave her there, so he caught her ankles and pulled, and another Mrs Hak-Tak so exactly like the first that no one could have told one from the other, stood beside them.

"Here's an extraordinary thing," said Mr Hak-Tak, looking helplessly from one to the other.

"I'll not have another Mrs Hak-Tak in the house!" screamed the old Mrs Hak-Tak.

All was confusion. The old Mrs Hak-Tak shouted and wrung her hands and wept, Mr Hak-Tak was scarcely calmer, and the new Mrs Hak-Tak sat down on the floor as if she knew no more than they did what was to happen next.

"One wife is all *I* want," said Mr Hak-Tak, "but how could I have left her in the pot?"

"Put her back in again!" cried Mrs Hak-Tak.

"What? And draw out two more?" said her husband. "If two wives are too many for me, what should I do with three? No! No! No!" He stepped back quickly as if he was stepping away from three wives and missing his footing, lo and behold, he fell into the pot!

Both Mrs Hak-Taks ran and caught an ankle and pulled him out and set him on the floor, and there, Oh, mercy, was another pair of legs kicking in the pot. Soon another Mr Hak-Tak, so exactly like the first that no one could have told one from the other, stood beside them.

Now the old Mr Hak-Tak liked the idea of his double no more than Mrs Hak-Tak had liked hers. He stormed and raged and scolded his wife for pulling him out of the pot, while the new Mr Hak-Tak sat down on the floor beside the new Mrs Hak-Tak and looked as if, like her, he did not know what was going to happen next.

The old Mrs Hak-Tak had a very good idea.

"Listen, my dear husband," she said, "now, do stop scolding and listen, for it is really a good thing that there is a new one of you as well as a new one of me. It means that you and I can go on in our usual way, and these new people, who are ourselves and yet not ourselves, can set up house next door to us."

And that is what they did. The old Hak-Taks built themselves a fine new house with the money from the pot, and they built one just like it next door for the new couple. They lived together in the greatest friendliness, because as Mrs Hak-Tak said, "The new Mrs Hak-Tak is really more than a sister to me, and the new Mr Hak-Tak is really more than a brother to you."

The other neighbours were very surprised, both at the sudden wealth of the Hak-Taks and at the new couple who resembled them so strongly that they must, they thought, be very close relations of whom they had never heard before. They said, "It looks as though the Hak-Taks, when they so unexpectedly became rich, decided to have two of everything, even of themselves, to enjoy their money more."

ALICE RITCHIE

ONE LITTLE, TWO LITTLE

Once upon a time there were one little, two little, three little, four little, five little, six little boys.

One little boy said, "Let's all live together."

Two little boy said, "We'll build a little house."

Three little boy said, "By the side of a wood."

Four little boy said, "On the banks of a stream."

Five little boy said, "We'll make ourselves a garden."

And six little boy said, "And no one shall bother us, and we shall look after ourselves."

So off they went and found a wood with a stream running by and room for a garden.

"Here we will build it," said one little, two little, three little, four little, five little, six little boys.

So they went in the wood and cut down one little, two little, three little, four little, five little, six little trees.

And they cut the trees into planks, and they nailed the planks together.

And they made one little, two little, three little, four little walls.

And one little floor for the upstairs, and one little floor for the downstairs, and one little staircase to go up and down by.

They put one little roof on the top with one little, two little, three little, four little, five little, six little chimneys.

They made one little door in the back and one little door in the front.

Inside the house they made one little, two little, three little, four little, five little,

six little rooms downstairs, and one little, two little, three little, four little, five little, six little rooms upstairs and each little room had two little windows so what a lot of windows that made.

And besides all this they made one little kitchen, and one little scullery, and one little bathroom and one little lavatory. And that is all they made inside the house.

But outside they made one little shed for the wood, and one little shed for the coal, and one little shed for the gardening tools, and one little pump to pump water from the river.

And when they had done they went back to the wood, and there they cut down, one little, two little, three little, four little, five little, six little trees.

And they sawed the trees into planks.

And each little boy made a little table.

And each little boy made a little chair.

And each little boy made a little bed.

And each little boy made a little cupboard.

Then they went to the town and went in a shop.

And each little boy bought a little plate.

And each little boy bought a little cup.

And each little boy bought knife and fork and spoon.

And each little boy bought blankets for his bed.

And each little boy bought everything he needed to make himself comfortable.

Can *you* think of something they bought in the shop?

Well, when they had done they went home to their house, and arranged all their things and lit one little, two little, three little, four little, five little, six little fires.

And one little, two little, three little, four little, five little, six little boys sat down beside the fire and each one said to himself:

"How lucky I am in my own little house, by my own little fire, in my own little room with no one to bother me and everything I need."

But all at once, WHAT a noise!

MIAAOOOW WOOOOW. MIAOOOUUULLLL YIAOUL.

They ran to the door and opened it a tiny bit.

In ran one little, two little, three little, four little, five little, six little cats, and each one as black as the middle of the night.

Each little cat ran into each little room and sat itself down by each little fire, and began to wash itself as cool as a cucumber.

And each little boy said, "I never thought of that. How nice to have company when I sit beside the fire."

And one little, two little, three little, four little, five little, six little boys gave one little, two little, three little, four little, five little, six little cats, one big, two big, three big, four big, five big, six big saucers of milk.

Then each little boy went back to his fire, and sat down beside it and the cats began to purr.

But all at once WHAT a noise!

BOW WOW WOW WOW WOOF WHOOOUUUFFF WOOOOW WOOOOOW WOW.

They ran to the door and opened it a tiny bit.

In ran, one little, two little, three little, four little, five little, six little dogs, and each one as white and woolly as a lamb.

Each little dog ran into each little room and sat itself down by each little fire, and began to scratch itself as cool as a cucumber.

And each little boy said, "I never thought of that. How nice to have company when I go for a walk."

And one little, two little, three little, four little, five little, six little boys, gave one little, two little, three little, four little, five little, six little dogs, one big, two big, three big, four big, five big, six big bones.

Then each little boy went back to the fire and sat down beside it and the cat sat on one side and the dog on the other.

But all at once WHAT a noise!

BANG BANG, BOOO HOOOOO. OH DEAR, BANG BANG.

They ran to the door and opened it a tiny bit.

One Little, Two Little

Standing at the door afraid to come in were one little, two little, three little, four little, five little, six little girls.

One little girl said, "We are lost."

Two little girl said, "Will you take us in?"

Three little girl said, "We are cold."

Four little girl said, "And hungry."

Five little girl said, "And frightened."

Six little girl said, "And have nowhere to go, so please will you be kind to us?"

One little boy said, "Come in."

Two little boy said, "Do not cry."

Three little boy said, "The fires are alight."

Four little boy said, "Supper is nearly ready."

Five little boy said, "No one shall hurt you."

Six little boy said, "You can stay with us forever. You can share our little house with us and tomorrow we will get you everything you need."

So in ran one little, two little, three little, four little, five little, six little girls, and each one as pretty as the morning.

And each little girl ran into each little room and sat herself down by each little fire and began to warm her hands as happy as you please.

And each little boy said, "I never thought of that. How nice to have a companion to play with and help in the work."

And one little, two little, three little, four little, five little, six little boys gave one little, two little, three little, four little, five little, six little girls one big, two big, three big, four big, five big, six big suppers.

And what did they have for supper?

Well, you must tell me that, because they had for supper the nicest thing you can think of.

And there they all stayed and lived happily ever after, one little, two little, three little, four little, five little, six little boys with their one little, two little, three little, four little, five little, six little cats; and their one little, two little, three little, four little, five little, six little dogs; and the one little, two little, three little, four little, five little, six little girls who helped to cook and clean and sew, and looked after the house while the boys were digging in the garden.

DIANA ROSS

THE WOODEN BABY

A man and his wife lived in a little cottage at the end of a village close to the forest. They were very poor; the man hired himself out by the day and the woman spun flax and sold it; yet they kept on saying: "If only we had a baby!"

"Be glad God hasn't sent you one," other folk said to them, "you've hardly enough to eat yourselves."

But the man and his wife said: "If there's enough for us, there would be enough for our baby—if only we had one!"

One morning the man was cutting wood in the forest, and he cut a log which was just the shape of a baby: head, body, arms, legs. He only had to shape the head a little to make it round and smooth, and trim the roots on its arms and legs to make them look like fingers and toes, and it was like a real baby, only it didn't cry! The man took it home and said to his wife:

"Here you are! Here's what you always wanted—a baby! If you like it, you can bring it up as yours."

His wife wrapped the baby in a little goose feather quilt, rocked it in her arms and sang:

> "Lullabye, lullabye,
> Little wooden baby boy.
> When you wake, my little sweet,
> You shall have some pap to eat.
> Lullabye, lullabye."

All at once the baby began to wriggle about in the feather quilt. He turned his head and began to shout:

"Mummy, I want something to eat!"

The woman was so delighted, she didn't know whether she was on her head or her heels. She laid the baby down on the bed and went to cook him some porridge. When she had cooked it, the wooden baby gobbled it all up, and as soon as he had finished he began to shout again:

"Mummy, I want something to eat!"

"Wait a minute, darling, I'll get you something at once!" She ran to a neighbour's and fetched a pitcher full of milk. The baby drank it up in one gulp, and as soon as he had finished, he began shouting for something more to eat. The woman was very astonished. "Why, baby, haven't you had enough yet?" She went out and borrowed a big loaf of bread in the village, brought it home and laid it on the table; then she went out again to draw water to set on the fire for soup. She had hardly left the room when the wooden baby, seeing the bread on the table, wriggled out of the quilt and jumped on the table; in a moment he had gobbled up the loaf and began shouting:

"Mummy, I want some more to eat!"

His mother came back to make the breadcrumbs for the soup. She looked round for the loaf, and it was gone! In the corner stood the wooden baby as fat as a barrel, rolling his eyes at her.

The Wooden Baby

"God preserve us, baby! You've never eaten the whole loaf?"

"Yes, I did, Mummy—and I'll eat you too!" He opened his mouth, and before his mother knew what was happening, she was inside him.

Presently the father came home, and as soon as he set foot inside the door, the wooden baby called:

"Daddy, I want something to eat!"

The father was startled, seeing before him a body as big as a stove, which opened its mouth and rolled its eyes. And recognizing the wooden baby, he said:

"The Devil take you! Where's your Mother?"

"I ate her up—and I'll eat you too!" He opened his mouth, and in a trice he had his father inside him.

But the more the wooden baby ate, the greedier he grew. There was nothing worth eating left in the cottage, so he went out into the village to look for something.

He met a little girl wheeling a barrow full of clover from the field.

"Whatever have you been eating to get such a big round tummy?" she asked. The wooden baby answered:

> "I've eaten, I've gobbled:
> A pot full of porridge,
> A pitcher of milk,

The Wooden Baby

A loaf of bread,
My mummy, my daddy—
And I'll eat you too!"

He sprang forward, and the little girl and her barrow disappeared inside him. Then he met a peasant bringing a load of hay from the meadow. The wooden baby stood in the middle of the road, and the horse stopped.

"Can't you move out of the way, you little monster?" shouted the peasant. "If I get after you——" and he cracked his whip. But the wooden baby took no notice and began again:

"I've eaten, I've gobbled
A pot full of porridge,
A pitcher of milk,
A loaf of bread,
My mummy, my daddy,
A girl with some clover—
And I'll eat you too!"

And before the peasant knew what was happening, he and his horse and cart were inside the wooden baby.

Then he went on. He passed a field where a swineherd was tending his pigs. The wooden baby licked his lips and gobbled up all the pigs and the swineherd on top of them; not a trace was left to show that they had ever been there. The wooden baby went on till he came to the foothills of the mountain, and there he saw a shepherd with a flock of sheep.

The Wooden Baby

"As I've eaten so much already," he said to himself, "I may as well eat you too!" He stuffed them all inside him: the sheep, the shepherd, and even the sheep dog, Boris. Then he staggered along further, till he came to a field where an old woman was hoeing cabbages. Without thinking twice about it, the wooden baby began to pull up the cabbages and gobble them.

"Why, look at the damage you're doing, you wooden monster!" cried the old woman. "Haven't you eaten enough without gobbling any more!"

The wooden baby made a grimace at her and said:

> "I've eaten, I've gobbled
> A pot full of porridge,
> A pitcher of milk,
> A loaf of bread,
> My mummy, my daddy,
> A girl with some clover,
> A peasant with his hay,
> A swineherd with his pigs,
> A shepherd with his lambs—
> And I'm going to eat you too!"

He opened his mouth and tried to gobble her up. But the old woman was so nimble, she managed to fling her hoe at him and cut his body open right across. The wooden baby rolled over on the ground—dead. And now you should have seen! The first thing to jump out of the hole the old woman had cut in him was the sheep dog, Boris, after him came the shepherd, and after the shepherd the lambs came leaping. Boris rounded them into a flock, the shepherd whistled and drove them away towards home. Then a whole herd of pigs came hurrying out; the swineherd jumped out after them, cracked his whip and set off after the shepherd. Then came the horse, drawing the cart loaded with hay; the farmer picked up the reins, spoke to his horse, and drove off behind the swineherd towards the village. After him came the little girl with the barrow of clover. Last of all the man and his wife jumped out from inside their wooden baby, carrying the borrowed loaf of bread, and walked home together. But never again did they say:

"If only we had a baby!"

translated by DORA ROUND from a Czech folk-tale

THE CATS WHO STAYED FOR DINNER

One evening in spring, a man and a woman moved into a new house. Just outside their door there was a garden. It was a pretty garden, with flowers and grass and even a tree.

They were very happy, because it isn't easy to find a real garden for your very own, right in the middle of a big city.

The next morning, as soon as they woke up, they ran to the window to admire their garden.

But what do you think they saw? CATS!

They saw so many cats, they almost couldn't see the flowers, or the grass, or the tree.

Big cats, black cats, little cats, yellow cats, white cats, grey cats, kittens. Cats with spots, and cats with stripes. And every single cat was skinny, scraggly, scrawny and smudged with soot of the city. And every cat had fleas.

"Oh, dear!" cried the man and the woman. "There are so many cats in our garden, there isn't enough room for us."

They shouted, "Go away! Shoo! Go home!"

But the cats only sat and stared at the man and woman. They could not go home, because they had no home. The little garden was the only place they had to call their own.

All day the cats played in the pretty garden. They chased the beetles and the butterflies, and smelled the flowers, and climbed the tree, and played a game of tag along the top of the fence.

They had a very good time.

But the man and the woman did not have a good time at all. They wanted to sow flower seeds, and mow the long grass, and dig out the choking weeds, and rest in the sweet spring sun.

But with all those cats in the little garden, there simply wasn't room enough for them too.

That night, the cats disappeared. They went out in search of food.

Every night they had to look for left-overs that had been thrown away, for, since they had no home, they had no one to feed them.

The man and woman went into the garden.

They found a big hole under the fence.

"This is how those cats get in," they decided. "We will fill it in, and then we will have the garden to ourselves." They filled in the hole under the fence.

The next morning they woke up smiling.

They hurried to the window to admire their garden.

But can you guess what they saw?

YES! Cats!

The big cats had climbed over the fence. Then they had dug a new hole under the fence to let in the kittens that were still too little to climb so high.

Every day the cats played in the pretty garden. They would not go away.

The man and woman were the ones who had to stay away. They could only look at the weeds growing stronger and the grass growing longer. They could only look at the sun and their tree. They were most unhappy.

One evening the woman found that there was a bit of milk left over after supper.

"I may as well give it to those skinny, scraggly, scrawny cats," she decided. She poured it into a pan and put it in the garden. That was on Monday.

On Tuesday, she ordered a whole extra quart of milk from the milkman. By mistake, of course.

Do you know what she did with it?

On Wednesday, she bought too much chopped meat at the butcher's shop— another mistake?

On Thursday, she came upon an extra dozen eggs in her shopping bag. But they did not go to waste, for eggs are fine for cats.

On Friday, the mackerel in the market looked so firm and fresh that the woman completely forgot that they were having supper with friends that evening. She bought some mackerel and brought it home.

Then, of course, she couldn't throw it away—because she knew how cats feel about FISH.

"Now mind you," the woman warned the cats, "just because I give you food, you mustn't think I like having you here in our garden. I just happen to have bought this extra food by mistake."

The cats sat still and stared at her. Then they all CLOSED their big, round, yellow-green eyes.

On Sunday, it rained.

From their window, the man and woman could see the cats huddled together under the weeds.

"I don't have much to do today," the man announced. "I think I'll rig up some kind of shelter for those cats—just for something to do."

He made a tent of striped canvas and stretched it over a corner of the garden so that the cats would have a dry place to sleep.

"But remember," he scolded, "just because I've made a shelter for you from

the rain, you are not to think I like having you here in our garden. I just happened to have nothing else to do today."

The cats sat still and stared at him. Then—each one WINKED one big, round, yellow-green eye.

And so summer went slowly by.

The cats began to be not quite so skinny, scraggly, scrawny, because the woman fed them every day. They began to feel good.

And when cats feel good—as you've probably noticed—they begin to wash themselves. They washed and they washed, and they washed away their smudge of city soot. They washed so hard, they even washed away their fleas!

Then one day, winter came. All of a sudden, it snowed and the wind was wild. The man and woman stayed indoors, warm and snug.

The cats huddled together under the icicles in the little garden. The man and woman almost couldn't see them through the thick frost on the window. But they knew they were there. Because now they knew that the cats had no other place to go to.

"I think I'll do a bit of building at my work-bench in the basement," said the man. "Just to get some practice, you understand."

He worked all day, hammering and sawing. He worked almost all night, too.

The woman could not sleep for all the racket he was making. Bamm-Buzz. Bamm-Bang. Bang. Bang.

And she could not sleep in the quiet in between. Because then she could hear the mewing of the cats in the cold quiet of the snow.

In the morning she ran to the window.

What did she see?

Yes! Cats! But look! What else?

A row of tiny houses!

They went into the garden—the man and the woman. This time he did not shout and stamp. This time she did not scold and swish her apron.

This time they said, "At first we did not want you here. But now we must admit that we've come to like having you for our very own. We know now that there is room for all of us in this pretty garden."

The cats sat and stared at them.

But this time their big, round, yellow-green eyes—SMILED!

PHYLLIS ROWAND

RAINY DAY

Here is a tale of four umbrellas. They lived in a wooden stand in the hall, between the window and the front door. The grandest of them all was Mother's Umbrella. She was tall, with a lovely curved handle for a head, and a beautiful blue silk dress, slim and tightly folded. She even had a blue silk jacket to match, with a frill round the top and a tassel. Mother's Umbrella was proud of her tassel. To tell the truth she was rather pleased with herself in every way, and the others sometimes became a little tired of her pride and her boasting. Still, she was very beautiful, and told them so many tales of the interesting places she visited, that they made the best of it.

Rainy Day

Beside her in the stand was Father's Umbrella. He, too, had a very fine curved handle for a head, and a well-cut black, silk suit. He didn't talk as much as Mother's Umbrella, but now and then he told them in his deep, slow voice about his journeys to the city in the train, and about the office where he waited all day until Father was ready to come home again.

In front of these two in the stand was Sally's Umbrella. Like Sally herself, she was small and short. But her head was quite different! It was a round, polished knob. Her dress was pale green and had little silver fishes all over it.

"Very pretty," admitted Mother's Umbrella. "Though I fear that unless Sally takes very great care of you, your dress will soon become shabby."

The little green umbrella only laughed. She said she really didn't mind a bit because she *knew* her owner would look after her.

"Why, only yesterday," she told them, "when Sally held me over her head she said I was the prettiest umbrella she had ever seen. She said that she loved my silver fishes. They made her feel as if she was walking underneath the sea."

"That's all very well," said Father's Umbrella, slowly, "but people are very forgetful, especially about umbrellas."

"I somehow don't think anyone would forget *me*," declared Mother's Umbrella.

A sleepy, rather cracked voice came from the back of the stand.

"When you're as old as I am," it said, "you'll know that anything can happen."

It was Aunt Jane's Umbrella who spoke. She had been standing there for longer than any of them could remember. The silver on her curved head needed polishing and her black dress, which was dull and dusty, had a big tear in it. Many, many years ago Aunt Jane had gone away and left her there, and now nobody ever took her out nor paid her the slightest attention. This wasn't very pleasant for her, of course, and she just stood there getting more and more miserable every year.

"Once I was as smart as any of you," she said, "and I went out almost every day. Ladies didn't put hoods and scarves on their heads when I was a young thing. Aunt Jane always wore a hat and she always carried me when she went out."

"*Really!*" said Mother's Umbrella, glancing at the old umbrella's torn and dusty dress.

"Extraordinary," said Father's Umbrella.

"You didn't have a pretty, green dress with silver fishes on it, did you?" asked Sally's Umbrella.

"In my young days a lady's umbrella always wore black, my dear. We didn't dress ourselves up to look like sunshades."

Rainy Day

One morning the sky was very grey, and even before breakfast the raindrops began to fall. At first they dropped slowly. Pit . . . pat . . . pit . . . pat, they went. Then they fell faster: Pit-pat-pit-pat. By the time breakfast was over, they were falling very fast indeed. Pitter-patter-pitter-patter, they went, splashing on the ground and making puddles in the road.

"It's an umbrella day today," said Father, taking the big, smart, black one from the stand. He opened it carefully outside the front door. And down the road to the station and the train and the office in the city went Father's Umbrella.

Soon two little girls called at the house for Sally on their way to school.

"I must bring my umbrella," she said.

"Oh, no!" they cried. "You're wearing your raincoat and hood. You don't want anything else."

"Oh yes, I do!" She took the little green one out of the stand and opened it outside the front door. And down the road to school went Sally's Umbrella.

Still the rain fell steadily . . . pitter-patter-pitter-patter . . . and when Mother came downstairs in her new coat and hat she said: "I must certainly take my

umbrella today." She lifted the beautiful, blue silk one out of the stand, and after removing the jacket she opened it outside the front door. It looked like a lovely blue flower. And down the road to the bus stop and the shops went Mother's Umbrella.

Only Aunt Jane's Umbrella was left in the stand. It was always like that. Sighing a long sigh, she went off to sleep, and it was afternoon before she woke up. Sunshine was streaming through the window into the hall, but it didn't make Aunt Jane's Umbrella any happier. "It only shows up the dust on my dress," she thought, sadly. "I've almost forgotten what the world outside looks like."

"Very nice indeed now," said the little green umbrella, whom Sally had just brought home. "The rain freshened me up beautifully and then the sun dried me."

Father's Umbrella was the next one to return to the stand. "I had a good bath this morning on the way to the office," he told the other two. "I got a little creased in the train, but I soon dried out. Mother's Umbrella should be home soon. She has been away a long time today."

"Mother herself is home," said the little green umbrella. "I can hear Sally talking to her. Listen!"

They all listened carefully, and this is what they heard.

"I don't know *where* I can have left it," came Mother's voice. "I've thought and thought."

Rainy Day

"Perhaps you left it in one of the shops, my dear." That was Father's voice.

"Or perhaps you left it in the bus." That was Sally's voice.

"I only wish I could remember," sighed Mother. "It was such a beautiful one."

The three umbrellas in the stand were worried, too. What could have happened to Mother's Umbrella? Although she was sometimes a little boastful and proud, she was one of the family after all, and it was dreadful not to know where she was.

The next morning the weather was bad again. Rain beat against the window in the hall: Pit-pat-pit-pat-pit-pat. Father's Umbrella said: "I see I shall be going to the office again today." "And I shall be going to school," said Sally's Umbrella. But what was Mother going to do without an umbrella at all?

Aunt Jane's Umbrella didn't say a word. Deep down in her old and dusty heart there was a big wish. If only Mother would take *her*! But then she looked at her shabby, old dress with the big tear in it and she knew that nobody could possibly want to take her out.

Off went Father's Umbrella to the station. Off went Sally's Umbrella to school. Mother said: "I must wear my raincoat and hood today when I go to town. Oh, I do hope I'm able to find my blue umbrella." She was just going out of the front door when she noticed Aunt Jane's Umbrella at the back of the stand.

"I suppose I couldn't . . . no, of course, I couldn't . . . wait a moment, though . . ."

Mother took Aunt Jane's Umbrella out of the stand and opened it. "Oh dear, oh dear!" she said, as she saw the dust fly out, and "Oh dear, oh dear!" as she noticed the big tear. "All the same, it's a very nice handle." Mother stroked it while she went on thinking. "I know, I'll take it to the little shop by the bus stop and get them to make it a new cover. I may as well hold it up on my way down there, for it will keep *some* of the rain from my face."

And down the road AT LAST went Aunt Jane's Umbrella!

There was great excitement in the stand in the hall that evening, for when the smart black and the small green umbrellas returned they found two surprises. Mother's Umbrella had come home! But Aunt Jane's Umbrella had gone!

"You can't think what a time I've had," cried Mother's Umbrella. "The things that have happened to me! Left in a bus! Taken to a big room and flung . . . yes, my dears, simply *flung* down on a counter! Bundled into a heap with a lot of strange umbrellas! A label tied round my neck!"

"Who were all the strange ones?" asked Sally's Umbrella.

"Oh, just poor things who had been left behind in buses and trains, you know. They all wanted to tell what had happened to them. I could scarcely hear myself speak."

Rainy Day

"You must have been glad to see Mother this afternoon," said Father's Umbrella.

"I was, indeed. 'That's mine,' she cried, 'that nice blue one.' Oh, but I'm glad to be home again! I'm quite worn out. At least, not *really* worn out," she giggled, glancing to the back of the stand where Aunt Jane's Umbrella always stood. "My goodness! Where is she? Where's Aunt Jane's?"

"Gone to a shop to be given a new dress," Father's Umbrella explained.

"Dear me!" said Mother's Umbrella, "how very odd!"

It must have been about a week later that Aunt Jane's Umbrella came back. Anyway, she said she was Aunt Jane's Umbrella, but it was hard to recognize her. The silver on her handle was bright and polished, and she wore a wonderful, new dress of red silk. It was as slim and tightly folded as the blue one belonging to Mother. Even her voice sounded less sleepy and cracked.

"Well, how do you like me?" she asked them. "I've a feeling I shall be going out more now. Do you mind making room at the front of the stand, please?"

Mother's Umbrella moved along a little way. She was so surprised by the way Aunt Jane's Umbrella looked and behaved that she could scarcely speak. At last she found her voice and said softly: "That's a very nice dress you're wearing, dear. A lovely shade of red. I do hope, though, that nobody mistakes you for a *sunshade*."

Aunt Jane's Umbrella laughed happily. "I shan't mind a bit," she declared, "as long as somebody takes me out."

Doris Rust

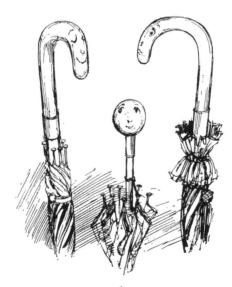

THE BAKER MAN

Mick and Mandy were in the kitchen. Mick's Mummy was out.

"Did you hear the door-bell ring?" asked Mandy suddenly.

"Yes," said Mick. "I'll go."

"No, let me open the door," cried Mandy.

They raced each other to the front door.

"It's the baker man," Mick cried. "Hullo, baker man!"

"Is your Mummy in?" asked the baker.

"No," said Mick. "She has gone to the shops. Can I help you?"

"Perhaps you can," said the baker. "How much bread does your mother want?"

"I don't know," said Mick.

"Then I'll leave you one large white," said the baker.

The baker took the bread out of his big basket, and he gave it to Mick.

"Let's put the bread on the table in the kitchen," said Mandy.

"No, I don't think we will. I think I'd like to show it to Mummy right away," said Mick.

"But you can't," said Mandy. "She isn't here."

"Oh, perhaps she came home when we didn't know," said Mick. "Through the back door."

"Perhaps she is upstairs then," said Mandy.

So they climbed upstairs to the bedroom, and Mick kept the loaf of white bread under his arm. But his Mummy wasn't upstairs. He looked in all the rooms. Mandy looked in all the rooms, too.

"I know," said Mick at last. "Perhaps she's in the coal shed."

So they went to the coal shed. It was dark in the coal shed. It was so dark that Mick fell over on top of all the coal. Down went the loaf of bread.

"Now the bread is all black," Mandy said in a small voice. "What shall we do?"

"We'll wash it, of course," said Mick.

"Yes," said Mandy. "We'll take it into the kitchen and let the water run over it."

Mick had the loaf of bread under the tap when his Mummy came in.

"Dear me!" she cried. "What are you doing?"

"We are washing the bread," Mick told her. Then he told her all about the baker man and the coal shed.

"But now the bread is all wet," Mummy said at last. "We shall have to dry it in the oven."

Mick and Mandy watched as she put the bread in the oven.

"She isn't cross," Mandy whispered to Mick.

"No," Mick whispered back. "We didn't mean it, did we?"

"We shall have to cut away all the outside crust," said Mummy, "when we have it for tea, but never mind, it will be nice and hot."

And it was, too!

ANNIE M. G. SCHMIDT

GALLDORA AND THE SMALL REWARD

Galldora was a rag doll, just a home-made rag doll, with shoe-button eyes and a sewn-on mouth and black wool hair, but though she was home-made, Galldora could laugh and sing and cry, in doll fashion, just as well as any other doll. One day Marybell, the little girl who owned Galldora, came into the nursery and said:

"Darling dolls and teddies, I've got a new pram, and I'm going to take you all out for a ride."

The dolls and teddies were delighted, and so was the small stuffed cat. In fact everyone in the nursery was pleased except Galldora. Poor Galldora sat on the window-sill with her head bowed very low, for she felt sure she would be left out of the treat. After all, she was just a home-made rag doll, and prams were very grand. Then, to her great surprise, Marybell picked her up and said: "You are coming too, Galldora; you look as if you could do with some fresh air, you look a little pale."

Me—me! thought Galldora, as she was pushed into the bottom of the pram. Me! Fancy not being left out after all! She was so thrilled that she hardly noticed what a squash there was in the pram as doll after doll and large and small teddy bears came piling in on top of her.

"Could you squeeze down a bit, Galldora?" a teddy bear said, quite kindly, and a large plastic doll said:

"I might be rather heavy on your leg, Galldora, but I'm afraid that's where I'll have to sit—there's nowhere else."

"That's all right," answered Galldora. She was in such a state of excitement. "Me—Galldora—in a pram!" She kept on saying to herself. Of course, she didn't see much because she was right at the very bottom, with all the dolls and the teddies on top of her keeping out the view, but she knew she was going along in the pram because she was jolted and bumped. Then there was an extra-bump, and—and nothing.

"Help!" squeaked Bobo, the stuffed cat. "I don't like this at all." The extra-large bump had bumped Galldora sideways, and there she lay, quite comfortably,

staring with one eye up at the chinks of blue sky that showed through the arms and legs and ears and clothes of the dolls and teddies on top of her.

"Oh, help!" the stuffed cat kept repeating in a very tiny little dry voice. "Oh, help!"

"Why, what's the matter?" asked Galldora.

"We're in the middle of a stream, and it's most awfully full of water, and, as everybody knows, water's very bad for cats."

"Are we sinking?" asked Galldora. She was quite unafraid, and merely interested.

"If we don't move very much," said the big teddy, "we'll be all right; the pram will be like a boat."

"The water's running past us, and it's making me feel dizzy," sighed Lulu, the walkie-talkie doll. "I feel ever so dizzy, ever so dizzy."

"But why are we here?" asked Galldora.

"Well," said a small white bear, "Marybell said the river would give the pram a nice wash, and she's gone off and left us. She's gone back for a scrubbing-brush and some soap, which she forgot."

Oh, well, I suppose she will come back, thought Galldora, and she stayed peacefully at the bottom of the pram, staring at the chinks of blue sky, and humming little tunes to herself. All the other dolls and teddies chatted away and tried to help Lulu get over her dizzy feeling, and the stuffed cat to get over his nerves. But Marybell didn't come back. She had forgotten all about the new pram. She had run off to play with her very best friend, Gay, and she stayed a long time with Gay, swinging on Gay's swing. Then she went home to tea, and it was not until she was splashing about in her bath that she remembered her pram. The splashing reminded her.

As soon as she remembered she grew very silent. She was so silent after her

bath and so very silent during her supper that at last her mummy asked: "What is the matter, Marybell?"

"It's got lost," said Marybell, not quite knowing what to say.

"What has, Marybell?" asked her mother.

"My new pram," said Marybell. "It's got lost in the stream," and that was all Marybell would say.

"But how could it get lost?" asked her mother. "And when did it get lost?"

"It got lost while it was having a wash in the stream," said Marybell. "It's got lost in the stream."

At last Marybell's mother went down to the stream to have a look, and she found the pram, lying on its side, right in the water, with the weeds and the tadpoles all floating in and about it. She pulled the pram out and set it upright, and then she fished about with a long stick and rescued all the teddies and the dolls that she could find.

"Well, I suppose that's the lot of you," said Marybell's mother, as she bundled them into the very wet pram, "there doesn't seem to be any more." As she spoke she trod on something soft. It was the stuffed cat. So she picked up the stuffed cat and put it into the pram with the others, and then had another good look round. There were no dolls, no teddies to be seen anywhere, just water and fish and weeds and green grass and kingcups and reeds. "Well, home we go," said Mary-bell's mother, and she pushed the dolls and the teddies and the stuffed cat home again. But Galldora was not in the pram. Galldora was a mile away, floating quite happily down the stream.

I am very thankful to that cow for bumping into the pram, thought Galldora, for this is really very nice. On and on floated Galldora down the stream in the golden evening. She watched the green fields slip past her and she watched the swallows as they darted low over the waters, seeking flies to eat. Now, this, thought Galldora, is one of the nicest ways of travelling. Of course, it's a bit wet, and I don't suppose the water will do my stuffing any good, but one can't expect everything. I really think it's even nicer than the pram-ride.

Away and away went the rag doll, with her red dress billowing out like a float about her, and her black wool hair streaming behind. Sometimes her head was under the water, and then she could be friendly with the fishes, and sometimes her head bobbed up over the water, and then she could have polite conversation with the dragonflies and the gnats. I wonder if this will go on for ever and ever? she thought. I really won't mind if it does.

But suddenly she was swilled round in a little eddy of water as it flowed swiftly from under a low iron bridge. The waters whirled her and some floating sticks up against great, smooth stones. To Galldora's surprise, there she stopped. Well, thought Galldora, I suppose I could be in a worse place—and now that I am quite jammed up against these stones, with the sticks all about me, it's not so likely that I will sink.

All that night Galldora stayed there, and she was quite happy, watching the stars and listening to the owls. It's all like a lesson, she told herself, like being educated.

Next day she found she did not lack for company. She was visited by an inquisitive trout who had a nibble at her shoes, and then a toad came and hopped

all over her, and decided she made a very nice sun-bathing place. Then a thrush came and had a tug at her eyes, thinking they were small snails, and later a cocky little chaffinch came and asked: "May I please, rag doll, have a piece of your nice hair? It will just do for my nest."

"Certainly," said Galldora, "just help yourself." The chaffinch did. He came back time and time again, and worried at her hair till she wondered if she would have any hair left. Thinking of nests, Galldora sighed, just one or two sighs, in a homesick way. I wonder, she began to think, if I will ever see all the teddy bears and dolls again, and my own special window-sill?

When the sun was high in the heavens a fisherman came walking along the river path, and stopped on the bridge. He leant there for a moment, gazing down at the cool, clear waters, and wondering about the fish. As he looked his eye was caught by a piece of red-coloured cloth, all muddled up in the pile of drift-wood against the big stones and the reeds. He went over and kicked it, in a wondering sort of way, with the toes of his boots. The red-coloured rag was, of course, Galldora, and the kick made her legs and arms leap about.

"Well, well," said the fisherman, "a rag doll." He bent down and picked Galldora out of the water and he wrung her out and he set her up on an iron spike on the railings of the bridge. "I suppose some little girl will be looking for you," said the fisherman, and being a kind fisherman he arranged Galldora very comfortably. He put the spike through the back of her dress and through the back part of her woolly hair, so that her face was right up, and she looked straight out and could watch all that was happening. Then the fisherman tucked her arms one into the other, so they didn't dangle down. Galldora thought the fisherman was the kindest person she had ever met. He had certainly taken a lot of trouble over her. She stayed there on the railings in the sun, smiling out on the world as she dried.

It was a lovely, all-alone place where Galldora was, and it was full of over-hanging green trees and mossy banks. The primroses shone there like stars, and, of course, it was just the place where birds felt very at home. So at home that they were all crowded up, and the nests were just everywhere. One lady robin, who had found all the holes and crevices already full of other birds' nests, came flying over to the bridge, and perched there, looking about for a home. As her bright, beady eyes were flickering this way and that, they met Galldora's bright, shoe-button eyes.

"Oh, dear, you do look worried," said Galldora.

"Yes, I am," said the lady robin, "very worried."

"What is the matter?" asked Galldora.

"Well, it's this way," explained the lady robin, "I can't find anywhere to make my nest. Everywhere is full up this year."

"Oh, could I—well, if you didn't think I was interfering—make a suggestion?" said Galldora timidly. The lady robin cocked her head on one side to listen. "You see my arms?" said Galldora. "They are tucked up aren't they?"

"Yes," said the lady robin.

"Well," said Galldora, still very timidly, "come and have a closer look." The lady robin flew over and, perching on Galldora's head, looked at Galldora's tucked-up arms.

"Why!" said the lady robin, "what a wonderful cosy place to make a nest. It's just what I'm looking for," and she flew away and came back a little later with her husband. At once they started to build a nest in Galldora's arms.

Now, some days later, the fisherman passed Marybell's house. Outside, on a little tree, he saw a notice hanging by some string, and the notice said: LOST—A

RAGDOLL. LOST IN RIVER. IF FOUND, SMALL REWARD. He at once rang the bell and told Marybell's mother all about Galldora.

So, that afternoon, Marybell and her mother went down to the lonely, greeny part of the river where very few people went, except fishermen, and there, on the bridge, just as they had been told, they found Galldora. There too they found in Galldora's arms a nest with four eggs.

Marybell's mother, who understood all about eggs and nests, took Marybell a little way away, and they both sat very silent on the river bank and watched. Quite soon the lady robin came flying straight to Galldora and sat in the nest. Marybell was so excited she wanted to jump up and pick up the eggs, but her mother said:

"No, Marybell, you will upset her, but we'll come every day to see the robins." So every day Marybell came and looked at Galldora and the robins, from a safe distance, of course, so as not to upset the robins. And every day, when she left, Marybell waved her hand at Galldora. And every day Galldora seemed to wink back.

Marybell was so proud of Galldora she said:

"You know, Mummy, I think Galldora is the cleverest of all my dolls. I think she must have the small reward that the fisherman didn't want." So Galldora, when the baby robins had grown up and flown away, and she had come home, was given the small reward, which was a diamond star brooch out of a cracker. And Galldora proudly wears it, even to this day.

MODWENA SEDGWICK

THE HAT

To the King and Queen of Salvatia was born a baby boy. At his christening many godmothers gathered about the royal babe to give him gifts.

"I give him beauty," said one.

"I give him courage," said a second.

"I give him fortitude," said a third.

"And I give him a merry heart and the boon of laughter," said another.

And when all but one godmother had given him gifts, this last one came slowly up to the King and Queen and said, "I have nothing for him now, but upon the day when he becomes King let him come to me, and I will bestow upon him a gift of great worth."

When the prince was twenty his father died, and he became King, and was crowned in the old cathedral with the title of Karol I.

As soon as the ceremony was over, King Karol drove in his state carriage to the house of his godmother, and there demanded the gift she had promised.

The godmother, now an old, old woman, bade him sit down, and going to an old cupboard, she took out a worn and battered hat. She held it out to him. "Here, O King," she said, "is the gift I promised you."

The King gave a cry of startled wonder. And then he flushed angrily. "It is a poor joke that you play upon me, godmother," he said.

"No joke, O King," replied the old woman gently; "it is in truth a battered hat, and a worn hat, and so it seems it would ill become a king. Yet no possession in all the world should be dearer to the heart of a true king."

The Hat

"Godmother," answered King Karol, "you speak in riddles and I cannot understand."

"Listen, then," went on the old woman, "while this hat is upon your head you will see the truth in all things."

"That is indeed splendid," cried Karol, "give it to me, and accept my warmest thanks."

"But," went on the godmother, raising a warning finger, "it is dangerous for you to wear the hat unless seeing the truth you speak it."

"Have no fear, godmother," laughed King Karol, "I will speak the truth always, let come what may."

Then the old woman gave him the worn and battered hat with her blessing; and warned him to tell no one of its magic powers.

With a nod and a gay laugh the King returned to his palace.

He told no one of the amazing gift, but he determined to wear the hat instead of a crown. And when the next day he sat upon the throne, with the old worn hat upon his head, and the golden crown upon a cushion at his feet, the people stared wonderingly at the strange whimsy of the new King.

And when he went through the streets of his capital in his carriage, wearing the battered hat, the people who gathered in thousands to cheer him, forgot to cheer, and turned from him to hide their smiles. And there were many who nodded and pursed their lips and looked down their noses and tapped their foreheads with deep meaning.

But the people of Salvatia soon found out that their new monarch was a wise one. When they came before him to hear his judgment or to ask his counsel, they discovered quickly that it was useless for them to lie, for the King pierced to the very heart of their tale, and dragged out the truth into the light of day.

And so King Karol became renowned for his wisdom, and his people were proud to be his subjects. Here and there, indeed, there were grumblers who said, "The King's judgments are too harsh; his speech is too plain; it ill becomes a young man to be so unkind, so cold, so cruel in his judgments." But as these folk were those who had tried to wheedle and cozen the King with lies, hocus-pocus and mumbo-jumbo, no one took any notice of them.

And then King Karol married the beautiful Princess Sabina from a neighbouring country.

And then Karol's troubles began; for the first time that Queen Sabina (as she was now called) saw him put on the battered old hat before descending to the throne-room, she raised her little hands in horror and cried: "My darling one, whatever is that?"

"That, my little sweetling?" laughed King Karol, "why, that is my crown. And a wonderful crown it is, for it is a hat also, and is equally suitable for palace or street."

"My precious!" gasped the Queen, with a pretty pout, "it's only suitable for the dustbin."

"Dustbin!" chuckled King Karol, "why, I wouldn't exchange this crown for the wealth of Asia." And doffing the hat for a moment to kiss her pretty eyes, he replaced it, and with a smile hurried down to the throne-room to begin the day's work.

But the more the Queen thought about the hat, the more she disliked it. And when that afternoon she drove out with the King through the city, she felt so ashamed, that when they returned home she burst into tears and refused to be comforted.

She covered one pretty blue eye with her kerchief, and ' ¦ed wistfully and beguilingly at the King out of the other. "You don't love me at all," she said, with a little sniff.

"My heart's delight!" cried the King, "I love you better than my life."

"Then let me burn that hideous old hat," she said eagerly.

"No! no!" cried King Karol hastily; "you do not know what you ask."

The Hat

Then as the Queen's sobs broke out afresh, he put his fingers in his ears, and hurriedly ran downstairs.

The Queen woke very early the next morning. She turned over and looked at King Karol sleeping peacefully by her side. She thought how much she loved him, and how happy they would be if only he would not wear that old and hideous hat.

Just then, out in the street beneath the palace windows, she heard a tinker crying his wares: "Fine kettles, lovely saucepans, marvellous pots and pans; they never leak, they never rust, they will last for ever and ever. Buy! buy! buy!"

A wonderful idea came into the Queen's head. She slipped softly from the warm bed, took the King's hat down from its peg, and hurrying quietly down the stairs, opened the side-door of the palace and beckoned to the tinker.

The tinker, who was a big, red-faced man with sandy hair and whiskers, came quickly to the door, doffed his cap, bowed low and said (not recognizing the Queen), "Pots and pans, lady, kettles or saucepans?"

"I'll buy three kettles," whispered the Queen, opening her gold-chain reticule, and taking out some money: "but you must do me a favour."

"Anything I can, lady," replied the tinker in his hoarse voice, "and thank you kindly."

"Will you, then," asked Queen Sabina, "exchange your silly old cap for this nice hat?" And she held out the old and battered hat of King Karol.

"The kettles are five golden guilders each," said the tinker, looking dubiously at the battered hat. He had heard tales of the King's hat but it never entered his head that this could be the one; indeed, he did not dream that he was speaking to the Queen, but thought she was some noble's daughter staying at the palace.

"Five golden guilders each!" said the Queen. "It seems rather dear, but I'll take them." And counting the money into his hand, she took the kettles, and then held out to him the old hat.

The tinker took the battered hat, and handing to the Queen his old cap, perched the hat jauntily upon his sandy locks and turned away.

Before the Queen could close the door, the tinker came back again. "One minute, lady," he said hoarsely, and with a strange look in his eyes, "how much did I say the kettles were?"

"Five golden guilders each," replied the astonished Queen.

"A lie, lady, a lie," muttered the tinker, with an abashed blink; " 'twas five silver groats I should have said." And he held out the money in his hand.

"No matter! no matter!" cried the Queen, who was eager to get back to bed before the King awoke. "Keep the money and buy your wife a silk dress." And she shut the door and, hurrying upstairs, crept into bed.

She awoke the King as she lay down beside him. "My darling," cried the King, "why you're shivering with cold. It's tea you want." And he rang the bell for their early tea.

As they sat up sipping their tea, there presently sounded from the street below the noise of cheering and shouting and noisy laughter.

"Bless my bed-socks!" cried King Karol, "whatever is all that racket?"

And then Queen Sabina heard the hoarse voice of the tinker raised above the tumult: "Old kettles," he bellowed huskily, "mouldy saucepans, rusty pots and pans; they all leak, rusty! rusty! rusty! and they won't last a week. Don't buy! don't buy! don't buy!"

"My precious," said the King, "whatever is that madman saying?"

"I—I—can't quite hear," stammered the Queen, "come drink your tea before it is cold."

But down in the street a vast crowd was roaring with helpless laughter. Men,

women and children were standing round the tinker holding their sides, screaming with merriment, and gasping for breath. The tinker, a strange look of wild surprise in his eyes, was bellowing hoarsely his queer but truthful rigmarole.

And then a gust of wind blew his hat away over the heads of the people, and a score of little boys started off in pursuit. "Roll up and buy!" bellowed the tinker hoarsely; "fine kettles, lovely saucepans, marvellous pots and pans; they never leak, they never rust, they'll last for ever and ever. Buy! buy! buy!"

At this the mirth of the crowd rose to a very babel of merriment. The tinker stared at the people in puzzled anger. "What? What? What?" he was beginning furiously, when a small boy squeezed to his side and handed him his hat.

With a nod of thanks the tinker clapped the hat upon his head, and immediately began to roar at the top of his great husky voice: "Hi! hi! hi! old kettles, mouldy saucepans, rusty pots and pans, they all leak, rusty! rusty! rusty! and they won't last a week. Don't buy! don't buy! don't buy! hi! yi! yi!"

At this the laughter of the crowd became an uproar. But suddenly the tinker clapped his hand to his head, snatched off the hat, and muttering to himself, "It must be the hat; it's bewitched," he broke through the crowd and set off at a run for the side-door of the palace.

There he battered at the door until the Queen slipped on her dressing-gown and hastened down the stairs. But the King followed her quickly, and as she opened the door, he stepped outside, and grasping the tinker by the collar of his coat, dragged him inside the hall, sat him in a chair, and said, "Now then, my man, what's all this?"

The tinker sat with the hat held behind him and looked first at the Queen and then at the King. Suddenly, guessing the truth, he held the hat to the King. "I've brought back your Majesty's hat," he said.

"My hat? my hat?" gasped the amazed King; "where in the name of magic did you get it?"

The tinker looked appealingly at the Queen. Sabina went up to the King; she put her arm about his neck, and hiding her head upon his breast, told him what she had done.

The King laughed. Then he turned to the tinker and said: "Tinker, can you hold your tongue?"

"Till I die," said the tinker.

"Keep my secret, then," said the King, "and here is something for remembrance." And he took a ring from his finger, and the Queen's favourite bangle from her arm, and handing them to the delighted tinker, dismissed him.

"And now, my heart's joy," said King Karol, "I'll try to please you a little. If I wear a gold band around my old hat, will that satisfy you?"

"Indeed, my own, it will!" cried Sabina joyously, and she kissed his nose.

But when the King came to wear the battered old hat with the golden band

round it, he found that the band weakened the magic, and that he now saw and spoke the whole truth only for twenty-three hours out of the twenty-four.

"Well! well! well!" he said to himself, when he discovered this, "we must have a little make-belief now and then." Then he laughed gaily, and sending for an artist, he made him paint in gold letters above his throne this couplet:

A tarradiddle now and then
Is relished by the wisest men.

STEPHEN SOUTHWOLD

HENRY AND STAR

One morning Henry was dozing at the end of the runway, when Sam, his pilot, came running across the grass.

"We must be ready for take off in a few moments, Henry," he called. "We've a special passenger this morning, and he's in a hurry."

Quickly Sam filled up Henry's petrol tanks, and checked his oil. Then he started Henry's engine, and a few moments later a large, fat man hurried towards them and climbed aboard.

"All right, pilot," he shouted, almost before he was in the cabin. "You can start, and I hope you'll hurry. I don't want to be late for my appointment."

Henry's little motor began to hum, his rotor blades swished, and up he went. He circled the aerodrome once, and set off towards the mountains.

He passed over the big town. Once again all the people looked up when they heard Henry. Then he crossed the narrow, silver ribbon that was the river, and ahead of him lay the mountains. He started to climb.

The mountains were very high, and the fat man was very heavy. Poor Henry began to feel very tired.

He struggled up, up, but the mountains still went higher and higher.

"I can't do it, Sam," he panted.

"Of course you can, Henry," said Sam. "You've done it heaps of times before."

"But never with such a heavy load," complained Henry. "This last bit is the steepest. I'll *never* get over it."

"Come along," coaxed Sam. "Try harder, Henry."

179

Henry tried and tried, but it was no use. "I must have a rest," he cried. "Only for a moment, and then I'll try again. I'll go down on that small strip of grass just below the top of the mountain."

He sank gratefully down, his engine throbbing painfully. But when his wheels touched the grass, there came a soft sucking sound, and he started to sink. The ground where he had landed was oozy, boggy mud. Poor Henry was stuck!

"Now what are we going to do?" yelled the fat man. "You silly little helicopter!"

"We'd better get out," said Sam. "Perhaps we can push Henry on to solid ground."

Sam and the fat man climbed out of the cabin. They sank in the mud, too.

"This is dreadful," moaned the fat man. "I shall be late for my appointment, and now my shoes and my trousers are all muddy."

Sam fixed a rope round Henry's nose, and he and the fat man pulled and pulled. Henry waggled his rotors and tried to jump. But it was no use. His wheels were stuck fast.

"I'm not pulling any more," declared the fat man. "He'll just have to stay there."

"Just once more," pleaded Sam.

"Stupid things, helicopters," grumbled the fat man, as they tried again. "Why ever didn't I go by train?"

"I'm afraid it's no use, Henry," panted Sam. "I'll have to go for help."

As he spoke, a dark brown mountain pony appeared out of the trees at the edge of the bog. Her name was Star, because she had a white, star-shaped mark on her forehead. Close beside her walked her colt, Prince.

"Why, Henry," she called. "What are you doing here? I've often seen you passing over the mountain. Why have you stopped?"

"I came down to rest, and I'm stuck!" wailed Henry miserably.

"I'll help you," said Star. "There's a path through the bog here. If Sam ties the rope round me, and we all pull, we'll easily get you out."

So Sam tied the rope round Star. Star pulled, and Sam and the fat man pushed, and, slowly, slowly, Henry's wheels came out of the mud. Star guided them on to the path, and soon he was safely on firm ground again.

"Thank you, Star," said Henry gratefully. "I'm sure I can manage now. Perhaps, some day, I'll be able to repay you for your help."

Sam and the fat man cleaned their shoes with handfuls of grass, and climbed aboard. Sam started Henry's engine. Up, up, up, he struggled, until with one final effort, he was over the top of the mountain.

"Good-bye," shouted Henry. "Thank you very much."

Star lifted her head and whinnied loudly.

One day, a few weeks later, Henry was once again flying over the mountains. This time he only had Sam with him, and he climbed easily. Just as he was passing over the top, he saw Star again.

When she saw Henry, she neighed and neighed, and started to rush round in circles.

"I believe Star's in trouble," said Henry anxiously.

"Do you think she's trying to signal us?" asked Sam, leaning over the side. "Go down, Henry, and we'll see what's happened."

Henry went down until he was hovering over the place where the pony stood.

"Is anything wrong, Star?" he called.

"It's Prince," moaned Star. "He's wandered away. I can't find him."

"We'll help you look for him," said Sam. "Where did you last see him?"

"I was nibbling at some especially tasty moss on the top of that cliff. I thought he was behind me, but when I turned round he had disappeared."

"We'll fly over the cliff straight away," said Sam. "Come along, Henry. Go very slowly, so that we don't miss Prince."

Henry flew very slowly up and down the cliff top. Star followed them, neighing unhappily. Suddenly she stopped, and her ears pricked. She neighed again, and Sam and Henry heard a very faint answering whinny. "It's Prince!" shouted Henry.

"I can't see him," said Sam. "Fly a little farther out, so that we can see the whole of the cliff face."

Suddenly they saw him. He was half-way down the cliff, on a ledge, half-hidden by the clump of bushes that had broken his fall.

"We've found him, Star," shouted Henry. "We'll bring him up for you."

Henry hovered over the top of the cliff, and held on tightly to the rope ladder, while Sam climbed carefully down. Star watched anxiously. She called out to Prince to be quite still. But Prince couldn't have moved. He was wedged tight. Sam fastened a rope round him and climbed back up the ladder.

Slowly Henry rose upwards. Up came the rope, with poor little Prince dangling at the end of it, too frightened even to struggle. Henry flew carefully towards Star, and put Prince gently down beside his mother. Sam climbed down the ladder again, and untied the rope. Prince snuggled up beside his mother and whinnied with joy. He was safe!

Sam examined him carefully.

"I'm sure he's not hurt," he said, at last. "No bones broken. He'll be all right now."

"Thank you very much," said Star gratefully.

"I'm glad we could help," said Henry and Sam. "It's the best way of saying 'Thank you' for the help you gave us. Prince will soon be as frisky as ever. Good-bye, Star. We'll come and see you again one day."

Sam climbed back into the cabin, and pulled the ladder up after him. *Swish-swish* went Henry's rotors, and they rose high into the air. As they flew away over the top of the mountain, Star wandered off among the rocks and trees, grazing happily, with Prince already kicking up his heels beside her.

DORA THATCHER

THE RIDDLE-ME-REE

> *"In marble walls as white as milk,*
> *Lined with a skin as soft as silk,*
> *Within a fountain crystal clear,*
> *A golden apple doth appear.*
> *No doors there are to this strong-hold,*
> *Yet thieves break in and steal the gold."*

Little Tim Rabbit asked this riddle when he came home from school one day.

Mrs Rabbit stood with her paws on her hips, admiring her young son's cleverness.

183

"It's a fine piece of poetry," said she.

"It's a riddle," said Tim. "It's a riddle-me-ree. Do you know the answer, Mother?"

"No, Tim," Mrs Rabbit shook her head. "I'm not good at riddles. We'll ask your father when he comes home. I can hear him stamping his foot outside. He knows everything, does Father."

Mr Rabbit came bustling in. He flung down his bag of green food, mopped his forehead, and gave a deep sigh.

"There! I've collected enough for a family of elephants. I got lettuces, carrots, wild thyme, primrose leaves and tender shoots. I hope you'll make a good salad, Mother."

"Can you guess a riddle?" asked Tim.

"I hope so, my son. I used to be very good at riddles. What is a Welsh Rabbit? Cheese! Ha ha!"

"Say it again, Tim," urged Mrs Rabbit. "It's such a good piece of poetry, and all."

So Tim Rabbit stood up, put his hands behind his back, tilted his little nose and stared at the ceiling. Then in a high squeak he recited his new riddle:

> "In marble walls as white as milk,
> Lined with a skin as soft as silk,
> Within a fountain crystal clear,
> A golden apple doth appear.
> No doors there are to this strong-hold,
> Yet thieves break in and steal the gold."

Father Rabbit scratched his head, and frowned.

"Marble walls," said he. "Hum! Ha! That's a palace. A golden apple. No doors. I can't guess it. Who asked it, Tim?"

"Old Jonathan asked us at school today. He said anyone who could guess it should have a prize. We can hunt and we can holler, we can ask and beg, but we must give him the answer by tomorrow."

"I'll have a good think, my son," said Mr Rabbit. "We mustn't be beaten by a riddle."

All over the common Father Rabbits were saying, "I'll have a good think," but not one Father knew the answer, and all the small bunnies were trying to guess.

Tim Rabbit met Old Man Hedgehog down the lane. The old fellow was carrying a basket of crab-apples for his youngest daughter. On his head he wore

The Riddle-me-ree

a round hat made from a cabbage leaf. Old Man Hedgehog was rather deaf, and Tim had to shout.

"Old Man Hedgehog. Can you guess a riddle?" shouted Tim.

"Eh?" The Hedgehog put his hand up to his ear. "Eh?"

"A riddle!" cried Tim.

"Aye. I knows a riddle," said Old Hedgehog. He put down his basket and lighted his pipe. "Why does a Hedgehog cross a road? Eh? Why, for to get to t'other side." Old Hedgehog laughed wheezily.

"Do you know this one?" shouted Tim.

"Which one? Eh?"

"In marble walls as white as milk," said Tim, loudly.

"I could do with a drop of milk," said Hedgehog.

"Lined with a skin as soft as silk," shouted Tim.

"Nay, my skin isn't like silk. It's prickly, is a Hedgehog's skin," said the Old Hedgehog.

"Within a fountain crystal clear," yelled Tim.

"Yes. I knows it. Down the field. There's a spring of water, clear as crystal. Yes, that's it," cried Old Hedgehog, leaping about in excitement. "That's the answer, a spring."

"A golden apple doth appear," said Tim, doggedly.

"A gowd apple? Where? Where?" asked Old Hedgehog, grabbing Tim's arm.

"No doors there are to this strong-hold," said Tim, and now his voice was getting hoarse.

"No doors? How do you get in?" cried the Hedgehog.

"Yet thieves break in and steal the gold." Tim's throat was sore with shouting. He panted with relief.

"Thieves? That's the Fox again. Yes. That's the answer."

"No. It isn't the answer," said Tim, patiently.

"I can't guess a riddle like that. Too long. No sense in it," said Old Man Hedgehog at last. "I can't guess 'un. Now here's a riddle for you. It's my own, as one might say. My own!"

"What riddle is that?" asked Tim.

> *"Needles and Pins, Needles and Pins,*
> *When Hedgehog marries his trouble begins."*

"What's the answer? I give it up," said Tim.

"Why, Hedgehog. Needles and Pins, that's me." Old Man Hedgehog threw back his head and stamped his feet and roared with laughter, and little Tim laughed too. They laughed and they laughed.

"Needles and Pins. Darning needles and hair pins," said Old Hedgehog.

There was a rustle behind them, and they both sprang round, for Old Hedgehog could smell even if he was hard of hearing.

Out of the bushes poked a sharp nose, and a pair of bright eyes glinted through the leaves. A queer musky smell filled the air.

"I'll be moving on," said Old Man Hedgehog. "You'd best be getting along home too, Tim Rabbit. Your mother wants you. Good day. Good day."

Old Hedgehog trotted away, but the Fox stepped out and spoke in a polite kind of way.

"Excuse me," said he. "I heard merry laughter and I'm feeling rather blue. I should like a good laugh. What's the joke?"

"Old Man Hedgehog said he was needles and pins," stammered poor little Tim Rabbit, edging away.

"Yes. Darning needles and hair pins," said the Fox. "Why?"

"It was a riddle," said Tim.

"What about riddles?" asked the Fox.

> *"Marble milk, skin silk*
> *Fountain clear, apple appear.*
> *No doors. Thieves gold,"*

Tim gabbled.

"Nonsense. Rubbish," said the Fox. "It isn't sense. I know a much better riddle."

"What is it, sir?" asked Tim, forgetting his fright.

"Who is the fine gentleman in the red jacket who leads the hunt?" asked the Fox, with his head aside.

"I can't guess at all," said Tim.

"A Fox. A Fox of course. He's the finest gentleman at the hunt." He laughed so much at his own riddle that little Tim Rabbit had time to escape down the lane and to get home to his mother.

"Well, has anyone guessed the riddle?" asked Mrs Rabbit.

"Not yet, Mother, but I'm getting on," said Tim.

Out he went again in the opposite direction, and he met the Mole.

"Can you guess a riddle, Mole?" he asked.

"Of course I can," answered the Mole. "Here it is:

> *A little black man in a hole,*
> *Pray tell me if he is a Mole,*
> *If he's dressed in black velvet,*
> *He's Moldy Warp Delvet,*
> *He's a Mole, up a pole, in a hole."*

"I didn't mean that riddle," said Tim.

"I haven't time for anybody else's riddles," said the Mole, and in a flurry of soil he disappeared into the earth.

"He never stopped to listen to my recitation," said Tim sadly.

He ran on, over the fields. There were Butterflies to hear his riddle, and Bumble-bees and Frogs, but they didn't know the answer. They all had funny little riddles of their own and nobody could help Tim Rabbit. So on he went across the wheatfield, right up to the farmyard, and he put his nose under the gate. That was as far as he dare go.

"Hallo, Tim Rabbit," said the Cock. "What do you want today?"

"Pray tell me the answer to a riddle," said Tim politely. "I've brought a pocketful of corn for a present. I gathered it in the cornfield on the way."

The Cock called the Hens to listen to Tim's riddle. They came in a crowd, clustering round the gate, chattering loudly. Tim Rabbit settled himself on a stone so that they could see him. He wasn't very big, and there were many of

them, clucking and whispering and shuffling their feet and shaking their feathers.

"Silence!" cried the Cock. "Silence for Tim Rabbit."

The Hens stopped shuffling and lifted their heads to listen.

Once more Tim recited his poem, and once more here it is:

> "*In marble walls as white as milk,*
> *Lined with a skin as soft as silk,*
> *Within a fountain crystal clear,*
> *A golden apple doth appear.*
> *No doors there are to this strong-hold,*
> *Yet thieves break in and steal the gold.*"

There was silence for a moment as Tim finished, and then such a rustle and murmur and tittering began, and the Hens put their little beaks together, and chortled and fluttered their wings and laughed in their sleeves.

"We know! We know!" they clucked.

"What is it?" asked Tim.

"An egg," they all shouted together, and their voices were so shrill the farmer's wife came to the door to see what was the matter.

So Tim threw the corn among them, and thanked them for their cleverness.

"And here's a white egg to take home with you, Tim," said the prettiest hen, and she laid an egg at Tim's feet.

How joyfully Tim ran home with the answer to the riddle! How gleefully he put the egg on the table!

"Well, have you guessed it?" asked Mrs Rabbit.

"It's there! An egg," nodded Tim, and they all laughed and said: "Well, I never! Well, I never thought of that!"

And the prize from Old Jonathan, when Tim gave the answer? It was a little wooden egg, painted blue, and when Tim opened it, there lay a tiny carved hen with feathers of gold.

ALISON UTTLEY

THE GREEN-AND-RED ROOSTER

Farmer Jones wanted a weather-vane, and when a pedlar came along he bought a green-and-red tin rooster and put it on the shed where he kept his hay.

One morning Miss Henny Penny was scratching around for worms when she happened to look up at the top of the shed. She dropped the big worm she had found and Speckled Hen picked it up and ran, but Henny Penny did not notice her, for she was standing with mouth wide open, staring at the green-and-red rooster on the top of the shed.

"Isn't he handsome!" she said, and she clucked and scratched, but the rooster on the shed did not lower his lofty head.

Henny Penny was a trim-looking little brown hen, around whose neck were a few white feathers which looked like a linen collar. She might have been called a tailor-made hen, so prim did she look.

Henny Penny walked up and down in front of the shed, and every now and then she cast a sly glance at the green-and-red rooster. He swung round a little, but never a glance did he give her. Henny Penny flew up to the fence and flapped her wings, then she walked up and down. She thought he surely would notice her there and crow, if nothing more.

"Oh dear," she sighed, "if only he would crow! I am sure he has a lovely voice." Still the rooster did not notice her.

"The wood-pile is higher," she thought. "I'll try that." So she flew to the top of the highest pile of wood. She walked about and flapped her wings, but the green-and-red rooster did not lower his gaze.

"He has the most beautiful comb I ever saw," said Henny Penny, more anxious than ever to attract his attention. A thunderstorm came up, and Henny Penny ran under a bush, but she made a peephole through which she could watch her sweetheart.

"He will fly down now," thought Henny Penny. The thunder rolled and the lightning flashed around him, but aside from moving back and forth he did not stir from the end of the shed. "Oh, isn't he brave!" thought Henny Penny, and when the shower was over she looked at him again. "How lovely his feathers look after the rain!" she said. "So smooth, and how they shine; any other rooster would look ruffled," and then she walked into the shed.

"Just to think," she sighed, looking at the roof, "he is just beyond those rafters."

Suddenly she flew up to a shelf on the side of the shed, from there she flew to the hay-loft, and after resting awhile up she flew to the rafters. She sat there looking at the window that was broken, just above her head. If she could get out of that she could reach her idol. She spread her wings, and, swish! she was out on the roof.

Henny Penny held her head down and scratched the roof with her toes, then she gave a sidelong glance at her idol, but he held his head high. She grew bolder and walked to the end of the roof; but she stepped back, her wings half spread, and her eyes looked as though they would pop out of her little head. "What!" she screamed. "My idol is tin, not only his feet, but all of his beautiful green-and-red feathers are tin."

Poor Henny Penny, she did not stop to go back the way she came; she went to the edge of the roof, spread her wings, and swish! thump! she was on the ground again. All the hens and rooster rushed to where she landed, their necks outstretched and making a great deal of noise; the pigs squealed and the dog barked.

Henny Penny jumped up and shook her feathers. "My goodness!" said the old grey hen, "whatever were you doing on the top of the shed? Do you want to break your legs?"

"I wanted to see the view from there," said Henny Penny, turning her head to hide her blushes.

"I think she went up to visit the weather-cock," said the white rooster, who more than once had tried to be friends with Henny Penny. "You'd better be satisfied with us live roosters," he continued, "and not fly so high."

Henny Penny walked away with her head held very high, but her heart was sad. "Anyway," she said to herself, "he is handsome, and if he were alive he very likely would love me."

ABBIE PHILLIPS WALKER

THE LAUGHING DRAGON

True was once a king who had a very loud voice, and three sons.

His voice was *very* loud. It was so loud that when he spoke everyone jumped. So they called the country he ruled over by the name of Jumpy.

The Laughing Dragon

But one day the King spoke in a very low voice indeed. And all the people ran about and said, "The King is going to die."

He *was* going to die, and he *did* die. But before he died he called his three sons to his bedside. He gave one half of Jumpy to the eldest son; and he gave the other half to the second son. Then he said to the third, "You shall have six shillings and eightpence farthing and the small bag in my private box."

In due time the third son got his six shillings and eightpence farthing, and put it safely away in his purse.

Then he got the bag from the King's private box. It was a small bag made of kid, and was tied with a string.

The third son, whose name, by the way, was Tumpy, untied the string and looked into the bag. It had nothing in it but a very queer smell. Tumpy sniffed and then he sneezed. Then he laughed, and laughed, and laughed again without in the least knowing what he was laughing at.

"I shall never stop laughing," he said to himself. But he did, after half an hour and two minutes exactly. Then he smiled for three minutes and a half exactly again.

After that he looked very happy; and he kept on looking so happy that people called him Happy Tumpy, or H.T. for short.

Next day H.T. set out to seek his fortune. He had tied up the bag again and put it into the very middle of his bundle.

His mother gave him some bread and a piece of cheese, two apples and a banana. Then he set out with a happy face. He whistled as he went along with his bundle on a stick over his shoulder.

After a time he was tired, and sat down on a large milestone. As he was eating an apple, a black cat came along. It rubbed its side against the large stone, and H.T. stroked its head.

Then it sniffed at the bundle that lay on the grass. Next it sneezed, and then it began to laugh, It looked so funny that H.T. began to laugh too.

"You must come with me, puss," said H.T. The cat was now smiling broadly. It looked up at H.T. and he fed it. Then they went on side by side.

By-and-by H.T. and the cat came to a town and met a tall, thin man. "Hallo," he said, and H.T. said the same.

"Where are you going?" asked the man.

"To seek my fortune," said H.T.

"I would give a small fortune to the man who could make me laugh."

"Why?" said H.T.

"Because I want to be fat," said the man, "and people always say 'laugh and grow fat'."

"How much will you give?" said H.T.

"Oh, five shillings and twopence halfpenny anyhow," said the man.

H.T. put down his bundle and took out his bag. He held it up near the man's face and untied the string. The man sniffed and then he sneezed. Then he laughed for half an hour and two minutes. Next he smiled for three minutes and a half.

By that time he was quite fat. So he paid H.T. five shillings and twopence halfpenny. Then he went on his way with a smile and a wave of the hand.

"That is good," said H.T. "If I go on like this I shall soon make my fortune." He tied up his bag and went on again. The black cat walked after him with a smile on its face that never came off.

After an hour the two companions came to another town. There were a lot of men in the street, but no women, or boys, or girls. The men looked much afraid. H.T. went up to one of them. "Why do you look so much afraid?" he asked politely.

"You will look afraid too, very soon," said the man. "The great dragon is coming again. It comes to the town each day, and takes a man and _ cheese. In ten minutes it will be here."

"Why don't you fight it?" asked H.T. "It is too big and fierce," said the man. "If any man could kill it he would make his fortune." "How is that?" said H.T. "Well," said the man, "the King would give him a bag of gold, and make the princess marry him."

All at once H.T. heard a loud shout.

"The dragon is coming!" called a man who wore a butcher's apron. Then he ran into his shop, banged the door, and threw a large piece of meat out of the window. There was now nothing in the street but H.T., the cat, and the piece of meat.

H.T. did not run away, not even when he saw the huge dragon come lumbering up the street on all fours. It crept along, and turned its head this way and that. Its face had a terrible look.

Fire came out of its nose when it blew out. And three of the houses began to burn. Then it came to the meat. It sniffed it and stopped to eat it. That gave H.T. time for carrying out his plan.

He took out his bag and untied the string. Then he threw it down before the dragon. On it came, blowing more fire from its nostrils. Soon the butcher's shop was burning. There was a noise like the noise from an oven when the meat is roasting.

The dragon still came on. When it got up to the bag it stopped. It sniffed. Then it sneezed so hard that two houses fell down flat. Next it began to laugh, and the noise was so loud that the church steeple fell into the street.

Of course it had stopped to laugh. It sat up on its hind legs and held its sides with its fore-paws. Then it began to smile. And a dragon's smile, you must understand, is about six feet wide!

The dragon looked so jolly that H.T. did not feel afraid of it any more; not in the least. He went up to it and took one of its forepaws into his arm. The cat

jumped on the dragon's head. And they all went along the street as jolly as sand-boys.

A woman popped her head out of a high window. "Take the first to the right," she said, "and the second to the left. Then you will come to the King's royal palace. You cannot miss it."

"Thank you very much," said H.T.; and he and the dragon and the cat smiled up at her. H.T. waved his hand. The dragon waved its other fore-paw. And the cat waved its tail.

So they went on—down one street and then another. At last they came to a big, open, green space in which stood a big palace. It had a wall round it with four

large gates in it. At each gate there was a sentry box. But not one sentry could be seen.

H.T., with his friend the dragon, came smiling up to one of the gates. Above the gate H.T. saw someone peeping over the wall. "He wears a crown," he said to the dragon, "so it must be the King." The dragon kept on smiling.

"Hallo!" cried the King. "What do *you* want?"

"Hallo!" cried H.T. "I want the bag of gold and the princess."

"But you have not killed the dragon," said the King.

"I should think not," said H.T. "Why, he is my friend. He is my very dear friend. He will not do any harm now. Look at him."

The King stood up and put his crown straight. It had fallen over one eye in his fright. The dragon went on smiling in a sleepy way. There was no fire in his nose now.

"But," said the King, "how do I know he will not begin to kill people again?"

"Well," said H.T., "we will make a big kennel for him and give him a silver chain. Each day I will give him a sniff from my empty bag. Then he will be happy all day and go to sleep every night."

"Very well," said the King. "Here is the bag of gold. You will find the princess

197

in the laundry. She always irons my collars. And you can have my crown as well. It is very hard and heavy. I do not want to be King any more. I only want to sit by the fire and have a pipe and play the gramophone."

So he threw his crown down from the wall. The dragon caught it on his tail and put it on H.T.'s head. Then H.T. went to the laundry and married the princess right away.

And the dragon lived happy ever after; and so did the cat; and so did everybody else, at least until they died.

I ought to tell you that King H.T. used the bag all his life to keep the dragon laughing. He died at the age of 301 years, one month, a week, and two days.

The next day the dragon took a very hard sniff at the bag. And he laughed so much that he *died* of laughing.

So they gave the bag to the dentist. And when anyone had to have a tooth out he took a sniff. Then he laughed so much that he did not feel any pain. And when the tooth was out he was happy ever after, or at least until the next time he ate too many sweets.

RICHARD WILSON

THE MAGIC WORD

Mother was baking a cake. She took out the blue bowl, the eggs and the egg beater. She took down the box of sugar, and the bag of flour, and the little brown bottle of vanilla from the shelf.

Then she lit the stove, and the kitchen was filled with a warm purring sound.

"May I lick the bowl?" asked David. He was sitting on the kitchen ladder talking to Mother, as he often did while she baked.

Mother looked mysterious. "There's a magic word," she said, breaking the first egg into the bowl, "and if you say it, you may lick the bowl, the spoon *and the egg beater.*"

"I'll guess," said David.

He watched his mother crack the second egg against the bowl. *What was the word?* He thought, and he thought, and he *thought.*

"ABRACADABRA!" he shouted.

198

"No," said Mother, whirring the silver loops of the egg beater around until there was a smooth golden-yellow mixture.

What was the word? David looked up at the spice shelf, and then he watched his mother flick some nutmeg into the cake. And he thought, and he thought, and he *thought*.

"HOCUS-POCUS!" he cried.

Mother smiled. "That's not the word," she said. And she sifted the flour and sugar into the bowl. It looked like a small snowstorm falling. She took the wooden spoon and stirred the batter around and around, until it clung to the spoon in a thick yellow sauce.

What was the word? David watched his mother drop three drops of vanilla into the bowl, and the sweet smell of the vanilla hung in the warm kitchen air. It was the smell of all the cakes in the world mixed up together.

And David thought, and he thought, and he *thought*.

"DOMINOCUS!" he shouted.

"Noooo," said Mother, buttering the silvery cake pan. "Not that."

Oh, what was the word? David leaned on the table, shut his eyes tight, and he thought, and he thought, and he *thought*.

"ALACAZIRCUS!" he tried.

Mother shook her head. "The word is much easier than that," she said. "Much, much easier." She opened the oven door and put the cake inside. Now there was a delicious, sugary, buttery, vanilla smell that made David swallow.

What was the word? He thought, and he thought, and he *thought*.

"Oh, please!" he begged.

His mother smiled. "There now, you've said the word!"

The Magic Word

"I said it?" asked David, very surprised.

"Yes," said his mother, "you said the most magic of magic words. It's——"

"PLEASE!" shouted David. And he laughed and his mother laughed too, as she handed him the bowl and the egg beater and the spoon.

CHARLOTTE ZOLOTOW

ACKNOWLEDGEMENTS

For permission to reproduce copyright material I am indebted to the following: the author and William Heinemann Ltd. for "Black Bill" by Ruth Ainsworth; the editor and Oxford University Press for "The Best House", "Phillipippa" and "The Three Rats" from *My Holiday Book* edited by Mrs Herbert Strang; the author and Messrs Methuen & Co. Ltd. for "Pete and the Whistle" from *Little Pete Stories* by Leila Berg; the author and Messrs Methuen & Co. Ltd. for "The Boy who growled at Tigers" from *Another Time Stories* by Donald Bisset; the author and Messrs Curtis Brown Ltd. for "The Travels of Ching" by Robert Bright; the author and The Bodley Head Ltd. for "The Little Red Hen" from *To Read and to Tell* by Norah Montgomerie; Messrs George G. Harrap & Co.

Acknowledgements

Ltd. for "The Little Half-Chick" by Sara Cone Bryant, "Galldora and the Small Reward" from *The Adventures of Galldora* by Modwena Sidgwick and "Milly-Molly-Mandy Finds a Nest" from *More of Milly-Molly-Mandy* by Joyce Lankester Brisley; the author and Highlights for Children for "Granny Blake and her Wonderful Cake" by Barbee Oliver Carleton; the author and the University of London Press for "The Tale of a Turnip" from *Stories to tell and how to tell them* by Elizabeth Clark; the Literary Trustees of Walter de la Mare and the Society of Authors as their representative for "The Hare and the Hedgehog" by Walter de la Mare; Ivy M. Dubois for her story "The Little Girl who changed her Name"; the author and Messrs Methuen & Co. Ltd. for "The Cross Spotty Child" from *My Naughty Little Sister's Friends* by Dorothy Edwards; the Society of Authors as the literary representative of the Estate of the late Rose Fyleman for "The Princess who could not cry" by Rose Fyleman; Charles Coleman Sellers for "Mrs Mallaby's Birthday" by Helen Earle Gilbert; the author and Brockhampton Press Ltd. for "The Great Hairy Unicorn" from *Mr Hare Makes Stone Soup* by Muriel Holland; the author and Messrs Faber & Faber Ltd. for "How the Polar Bear became" from *How the Whale became* by Ted Hughes; the author and Messrs Faber & Faber Ltd. for "Teddy's Old Coat" from *Tales of Teddy Bear* by Aaron Judah; Messrs Oliver and Boyd Ltd. for "How Bath Bun got his Name" from *Stories to tell to the Nursery* by Margaret Law; the author and the Oxford University Press for "The Fat Grandmother" from *Red Indian Folk and Fairy Tales* by Ruth Manning-Sanders; Messrs Curtis Brown for "The Magic Hill" by A. A. Milne; the author and Messrs Evans Brothers Ltd. for "Johnnikin and the Fox's Tail" by Rhoda Power from *Here and There Stories*; the author and Messrs Chatto & Windus Ltd. for "Two of Everything" from *The Treasure of Li Po* by Alice Ritchie; the author and Messrs Faber & Faber Ltd. for "One Little, Two Little" from *Nursery Tales* by Diana Ross; T. V. Boardman and Co. Ltd. for "The Wooden Baby" translated by Dora Round; Wonder Books Inc. for "The Cats who stayed for Dinner" by Phyllis Rowand, "The Magic Word" by Charlotte Zolotow, "The Old Iron Pot", "The City Boy and the Country Horse" and "The Little Grey Sheep", all from *Read Aloud Romper Room Stories*, copyright 1958, Wonder Books Inc.; the author and Messrs Faber & Faber Ltd. for "Rainy Day" from *All Sorts of Days* by Doris Rust; Odhams Press Ltd. for "The Baker Man" from *Love from Mick and Mandy* by Annie M. G. Schmidt, translated by Rose E. Pool; the author for "The Hat" by Stephen Southwold; the author and the Brockhampton Press Ltd. for "Henry and Star" from *Henry the Helicopter* by Dora Thatcher; the author and Messrs Faber & Faber Ltd. for "The Riddle-Me-Ree" from *Adventures of Tim Rabbit* by Alison Uttley;

Acknowledgements

the author and Messrs Hamish Hamilton Ltd. for "The Green-and-Red Rooster" from *Sandman's Farmyard Stories* by Abbie Phillips Walker; the author and Messrs Thomas Nelson & Sons Ltd. for "The Laughing Dragon" from *The Ever-Ever Land* by Richard Wilson.

Index of Authors